A Time
to Endure

Kyle Pratt

A Time to Endure
Camden Cascade Publishing

CamdenCascade.com

Copyright © 2014 Kyle Pratt
ISBN: 978-0-692-31759-4
First Edition – December 2014
All Rights Reserved

Editor: Barbara Blakey

Cover Design: Micah Hansen

DEDICATION

To my family, Lorraine, James and Robert, without their support this
would not have been possible.

ACKNOWLEDGMENTS

Writing is usually done alone, but creating a book is a cooperative effort.

Many authors say that their spouse is their biggest fan. My wife Lorraine most certainly is mine. This book would not exist without her support, ideas and constant encouragement.

I would also like to thank William Childress for beta-reading the manuscript

I owe a huge debt of gratitude to the members of my critique group; Robert Hansen, Barbara Blakey, Carolyn Bickel, Debby Lee and Kristie Kandoll. They are more than fellow writers, they are friends and mentors. In our weekly meetings I continue to learn the writing craft.

CHAPTER ONE

The frigid mud sucked the warmth from Caden's body. He moved close to the blackberry bramble for concealment. This ground was drier, but the thorns slashed his skin and scratched at his camo uniform.

On either side a soldier lay watching with him. Looking through the binoculars, he saw several Humvees and soldiers on the west edge of Hansen. He was certain more were just out of sight.

He shivered. *Two months ago I was promoted to Chief Foreign Policy Advisor for Senator Stevens. Now the senator is dead, the capital destroyed and I'm lying on the cold, muddy ground about to fight a battle in Washington state. Funny how things change in our lives.*

With the binoculars he scanned the forces arrayed against him. "They've been there for hours. Why haven't they made a move?"

The question was rhetorical, but one of the privates beside him shrugged.

As they continued to watch the convoy, the red-haired boy and girl Caden had seen often in the area strolled across the field to the stream carrying fish traps.

Caden froze.

The boy was in his late teens, the girl a year or two younger. Together they moved along the bank, and then put their traps in the water just twenty yards from the recon position. Afterwards, the two sat idly nearby looking in the direction of the trucks. *Go home kids.* But there was no way to communicate the message without exposing his position.

Caden pulled out his radio. "CW returning to unit." Watching the scouts, he whispered, "Keep watch on the convoy. When they move out, alert us." Crouching, he headed back around the corner with a silent prayer on his lips. *Please God, keep those kids safe.*

CHAPTER TWO

Zach's stomach growled as he pushed back his blankets. He turned on the lamp beside the bed and watched the steam of his breath rise into the cold air. There was no hurry. He knew that for him and his sister, Vicki, this February morning would be like all recent ones, cold and wet; a time to be endured as they labored to stave off hunger for another day.

The dawn had yet to peek over the horizon as the two teens rose from their beds and donned coats, gloves, caps and waders. Vicki stuffed the backpack with hot tea, smoked fish and other supplies as Zach gathered fish traps and nets.

"Leaving so early?" their mother asked, as she staggered into the room.

"It's time to go," Vicki said. "Are you okay?"

She slumped into a chair and shook her head. "I don't feel well."

"She's drunk, Sis. Did Bo find more booze?"

"Don't be disrespectful. I haven't had anything to drink for three days now."

Because you can't find anything. "Good. Come on, Sis." Zach exited the pastel blue, single-wide trailer that was their home.

The predawn glow provided enough light for Zach to lead his sister along the narrow path through the woods. He had walked this way many times, along the streams that flowed through the valley. Just visible under the canopy of cedar and fir trees were the ferns that dotted much of the forest. But this was not the lazy pastime of earlier

3

days. He would not have gotten up so early or on such a cold morning for fun.

Since the terrorists had set off nuclear bombs in Washington D.C., Seattle and other cities, people had bought or looted everything in the stores. Food was scarce and fish were now a primary source of nourishment and barter for his family.

Zach set down the wire mesh traps at the edge of the woods and pulled the cap lower on his head. He looked back at his sister and her long red hair. She often complained about the color or frizz of it, but right now he envied her well-covered ears.

In the distance Zach heard the rhythmic mechanical clatter of vehicle engines. Gas was rare and expensive so the sound of engines demanded attention. Sometimes he saw a police car and occasionally military trucks, but rarely a private car. The rumble came from the highway at the edge of Hansen, the nearby town. He picked up the traps and continued down the path. They were headed in that direction.

The waist high grass was thick and the trees thin as the two moved along a muddy path toward the stream. Zach saw the water now, but here it ran too deep for the traps. They would continue along the bank to another location, close to the highway.

It took only minutes to reach his favorite spot. The culvert where the water flowed under the road was fifty-feet farther downstream, but despite the road being nearby the only sound was the rippling of the water and birdsong from the nearby forest.

The creek was wide, but shallow. The fish preferred a narrow, deeper channel near the bank. That was where they would place their traps. Vicki knew the spot well and, reaching it, dropped the backpack on the bank. The two waded into the cold water each holding a wire cage.

Zach pushed a pole through the wire mesh of the trap into the silt below and then gathered rocks. As they worked to secure the first snare, the roar of engines returned.

"Do you hear that?" Vicki asked.

"I'm not deaf, Sis."

She stuck out her tongue and headed back to shore.

"Oh, very mature." Zach frowned. At barely fifteen she was a year younger than him and, in his opinion, still very much a kid. He bent low to weigh down the second cage with a few of the stones they had gathered. When the trap was secure, Zach sloshed to shore. He pulled a towel from the backpack and wiped the frigid water from his arms, and then held the warm thermos in his hands. He joined his sister in peering over the bank near the road.

The grass was low in the rocky soil along the highway and with Hansen located slightly uphill from them, he could see the road and three, maybe more, army trucks along it with smoke rising from their tailpipes. An American flag fluttered in the morning breeze. Why are they just parked there wasting gas?

Vicki slid below the bank. "We're done here; let's go on to the next spot."

Zach didn't look at her. "You go. I'll be along in a bit. I want to see what they're doing."

Vicki raised her head back over the edge and watched with him for several minutes. "I'm going to set the last two traps."

"Yeah, I'll be along in a minute."

As an orange sun topped the nearby hills, Zach counted more army vehicles, mostly Humvees and jeeps, parked along the highway shoulder. Nothing happened and he started to follow his sister, when a single Humvee rolled slowly down the road. He caught a glimpse of two people inside as it passed. Then he watched as it continued down the highway, around the curve, toward the lake. When he returned his gaze to the main group, dozens of fighters stood on either side of the road.

The troops moved into the field, like hunters flushing birds from bushes. These were American troops, but something told Zach to be cautious and unseen. He moved into the tall grass a few yards up the bank. He couldn't see as much, but if he remained still in his brown waders and a green shirt, he would be difficult to detect.

A Humvee raced back from the lake. Less than a minute later, a dozen truck engines started almost at once. As the seconds ticked by he heard the troops approaching.

Grass rustled behind him. Zach turned.

Two soldiers moved from the bramble on the far side of the stream. How long had they been there? They were dressed in the same uniform as the men coming down the road, but they stayed hidden in the shadow of the thicket. One soldier looked right at him. The man crouched lower and motioned for Zach to leave. The soldier reached into the bramble for something. Zach realized it was a radio.

A shot rang out.

The soldier collapsed back into the bushes.

The other returned fire and jumped for cover.

Zach wanted to run, but his legs refused to move.

The sound of gunfire became deafening.

The boy crouched low in the grass.

Dirt and leaves flew around the surviving soldier. Then he fell hard onto the first man and their blood flowed into the stream.

As the gunfire ceased, Zach's breathing was so loud that he feared it would reveal his position. He struggled to control it as he tried to understand the bloody spectacle just a few yards from him. Why were American soldiers shooting at other Americans?

Gun at the ready, another soldier burst from the tall grass.

Zach gasped.

Vicki appeared from nowhere and screamed.

The soldier jerked his gun in her direction.

"No," Zach shouted. "We're just fishing."

The man took a deep breath. "Hide," he commanded. "A lot of people will die today."

CHAPTER THREE

Grabbing his sister by the hand, Zach ran, splashing through the stream toward the culvert. As they hurried to the tunnel the current flowed faster and the waters deeper. They struggled into the darkness until they neared the middle. In the frigid waist deep flow he held his sobbing sister tightly. "Don't cry, Sis. We're fine."

Zach hoped his words were true. He prayed the water and darkness would hide them from other, less merciful, soldiers. "Why did you come back?" he whispered.

Still sobbing she said, "I saw them moving through the pasture and came looking for you." With each word her voice seemed louder. "I wanted to get you and go home."

"Shhhh. I know," he whispered.

"They shot those men."

"Shhhh. Sounds echo in here. We'll be okay," Zach whispered. "No one shot us."

Vicki buried her head in his shoulder as if to block out the world.

Seconds later trucks thundered overhead. With the noise, Zach felt free to move. First he wiggled his numb toes just to prove he could. They moved but the lower half of his body was stiff and cold. He shifted his weight and nearly fell. During a momentary pause in the vehicle traffic he heard gunfire, but it seemed distant. Looking through the far end of the culvert he saw a farmhouse with a barn beside it. *If we could get there we'd probably be safer and warmer. Even if we hid in the barn until the soldiers leave, that would be better than here.*

When the last of the trucks seemed to have passed overhead, Zach whispered to his sister, "I'm going to do a little scouting." Cautiously he stepped toward the far end.

"No, stay here."

"I'm just checking, I won't go outside." Looking out the far end he didn't see any soldiers. Gunfire raged, but now free of the culvert echo, he determined the shooting was far off.

As he looked about, his sister came up behind him.

Returning his gaze to the farmhouse he mapped out a route in his head. They could follow the stream for a few hundred yards and then, if they stayed low, the grass would conceal them as they approached the farm. They could get close without being seen by any remaining soldiers. "Sis, we're going to that house."

"No…no…please, let's stay here." She dug her nails into his hand.

"I'll lead." He pried her fingers loose. Keeping low, he moved with the water and caused barely a ripple. He then hugged the bank of the stream. He imagined he was hunting a deer and needed to get closer. The soldiers might not be hunting him, but he was certainly not the hunter. His heart pounded in fear and he crouched low to hide. Every step was slow and deliberate. He wished he had his bow. That would give him some ability to defend Vicki and himself, but it was back at the house.

It seemed to take forever, but when they neared another culvert, Zach saw an opportunity to head directly toward the farmhouse. Using rocks he climbed up the bank behind a large thicket of blackberry brushes. A rutted, dirt driveway split from the main road just a few feet ahead. Grass grew high along a fence that followed it. "Sis, stay low and follow me."

She nodded.

Confident they hadn't been observed, he moved away from the stream with his sister close behind. As they neared the home, the grass was cut low and cover sparse. He paused and looked about. There was a barn near the house with a car parked between, but nearest to them was an old tractor. He signaled his sister to follow him.

Crouching, Zach stepped from the grass-covered fence and heard the unmistakable rack of a shotgun.

He froze.

Vicki bumped into him. "Why'd you…."

Without moving his arms, Zach slowly turned his head and his eyes focused on the barrel pointed directly at him.

The young woman who held it stood behind a car. An older man stepped from the barn. He wore a green vest with many pockets and carried a black, military-style rifle. The front door of the home opened and another young woman holding a gun said, "What have we here, Maria?"

"I'm not sure," the other woman said. "Stand up you two and keep your hands in sight."

Zach stood slowly.

Vicki, white as he had ever seen her, followed with her mouth agape.

The man walked toward the brother and sister. A yapping puppy followed close by his side. "Quiet Nikki."

The dog slowed its barking.

Turning to Zach the man asked, "Were you trying to steal food? Are you hungry? Is that why you were sneaking up to our house?"

Zach was hungry. Since the first nuke attack a month ago it seemed fish was all they had to eat and not nearly enough. "No sir. We're doing okay. We just didn't want to be seen by the soldiers,"

The three holding the guns seemed to relax.

Zach took a deep breath. "They shot two men…."

Eyes wide, the woman with the shotgun demanded. "Civilians or soldiers?"

"Soldiers. If I hadn't seen it with my own eyes…what's going…."

"Show me where," Maria said.

Vicki grabbed his hand and held it tight.

"No Maria. I'm sure it's not Caden," the older man said.

The people huddled around the front porch discussing the pros and cons of going to find the two soldiers. Zach relaxed a bit now that the guns were not pointed at him. He turned and smiled at his sister. A hint of color had returned to her face. He looked back over his shoulder and considered making a dash into the field, but he was less afraid of the family than any soldiers who might still be there.

Returning his gaze to the three grownups, still debating what to do, he allowed his eyes to linger on the two women. The one they called Maria had dark hair and spoke like any other American, but her skin was a light golden-brown. He wasn't sure if her ancestry was Mexican, Spanish, or maybe even Italian. The other woman had brown wavy hair and pale white skin like most people from the area. They were both young and good looking enough that he could imagine dating either one but, being pretty much grown at sixteen, he was wise enough to know that probably wouldn't happen. Still, although he had a girlfriend, Zach's eyes lingered on the two women.

Suddenly he noticed the older man staring straight at him. Zach cast his eyes to the ground and stuffed his adolescent dreams to the back of his brain.

Two more women appeared on the porch and joined in the discussion. One was older like the man, perhaps his wife, the other younger and clearly pregnant. *How many people live here?*

The man walked to the edge of the yard and then stared through binoculars toward the main road. "There's a jeep near the intersection of Hops Road and the highway. I see three soldiers. There may be more."

"What if it is Caden, or David, and they're wounded?" the brown-haired woman said.

Finally, the one called Maria put up her hand in a stop gesture. "We've got to know for sure."

The pregnant woman nodded. "Wait a minute." She disappeared into the house and returned moments later with a green backpack and waders. She reached out the backpack to the brown-haired woman, but the old man took it.

"I'll carry the first-aid kit." the man said. "Lisa, you stay here and keep watch."

Brown-haired Lisa started to protest.

"I promise to tell you the truth whatever we find."

Slowly she nodded.

Maria put on oversized waders. "Come on," she said to Zach. "Show us the way." She started to leave while the old man struggled to get his waders on.

Zach didn't budge. "While I'm leading you back to the soldiers, my sister stays here and you protect her..."

"No, Zach don't go." She squeezed his hand even tighter.

"...and let her call our mom so she can say where we are and that we're safe."

The older woman nodded. "Of course she can call her mother." She turned to Vicki. "You look frozen would you like something warm to drink?"

Vicki nodded, but returned her gaze to Zach. "We're not safe. No one is. And what if Mom wants to talk to you? What do I say?"

"Tell her I'm outside. It's true and won't worry her much. I'll be back soon, and then we can go home." Once again he pried his sister's hand from his.

Still holding the shotgun, Maria approached Vicki and Zach with a gentle look on her face. Eyes on Vicki, she said, "We'll bring him back safe, I promise."

Zach's gaze fixed on Maria. "That's a big promise to make."

Dressed in waders, the man put the binoculars into one of his many pockets, adjusted the backpack and put the rifle sling around his neck. "Zach, take us back the way you came."

"Do I get a gun?"

The old man looked at the boy for a moment. "Do you know how to use one?"

Zach had gone on hunting trips with his father, but that had been years ago, when he was a kid. His father had carried the gun all those times and since his Dad died there had been no opportunities to hunt. "Point. Pull the trigger?"

"No, you don't get one."

With Zach in the lead, the three of them headed out. "Stay low along this fence. The tall grass will hide us."

As they neared the stream bed two army jeeps, followed by a flatbed truck, rumbled down the highway. Zach watched through gaps in the grass as they slowed and turned down the little road toward the farm. "Head for the gully and hide," he whispered.

Maria raced ahead and disappeared down the bank. Moments later Zach climbed down the rocky embankment to the water and looked for Maria, but couldn't find her. The man was the last to reach the stream. The rising ground on both sides restricted their view but, hopefully, also concealed them. As the vehicles approached, the two males splashed across the creek and crouched against the bank nearest the road.

When only the sound of the distant battle disturbed the quiet, they relaxed. For the first time since leaving the house they were free to stand erect. Zach looked downstream wondering where Maria was when he heard splashes behind him. Turning he saw her, soaked up to her hips, coming out of the dark culvert upstream.

As she came toward them, the man stood and stretched to his full height, wincing as he did.

Zach grinned at the sight. "I overheard Maria's name when you were talking back at the house. What's your name?" He resisted the urge to end the sentence with, 'old guy.'

The man caught his smile and said flatly, "Westmore." Then he seemed to look more intently at the young man, as if evaluating him. "Trevor Westmore."

The boy smiled. "I'm Zach Brennon."

Trevor nodded. "I've seen you and your sister fishing this stream and trading in the town market."

He stomach grumbled. He hadn't eaten today. "There's been no food in the stores for weeks. We catch, eat and trade fish to get by."

"I know," Trevor said. "We're all just trying to get by."

Maria hurried along the muddy bank toward the site of the shooting. The two men followed as gunfire echoed across the valley.

After walking several hundred yards in silence, Zach turned to Trevor. "I heard Maria mention two guys, Caden and David. Who are they?"

"Caden is my son and the commander of the National Guard armory in Hansen. Maria is his…friend…good friend. David is the XO."

Zach watched Maria trudge through the mud and freezing water twenty yards ahead of them and picked up his own pace.

"So why is the army shooting at the Guard?"

The old guy sighed deeply and seemed to consider the question as they walked on. Finally he said, "People in our own government and other countries are using the terrorist attacks to seize political and economic power."

Zach wasn't sure what economic power was, but said, "And your son is trying to stop them?"

"As best he can, yes, along with others."

The boy mulled it over. It seemed to him the old man was saying people at the other end of the country and foreigners were trying to tell them what to do. He didn't like that idea, but he wasn't even old enough to vote. As he walked along the stream bank he wondered what he could do to help, but nothing came to mind.

As they rounded the next bend in the stream the culvert under the highway came into view. He tensed as he remembered the shooting. Then his gut wrenched tight as the growl of many trucks filled the air.

The three hid side-by-side in the bramble and weeds as the roar reached a crescendo on the road just a couple of feet above them.

CHAPTER FOUR

The trucks rumbled by in a seemingly endless procession. The noise made it difficult to talk, Zach scooted close to Maria. "The two were shot just on the other side of the culvert."

"I've got to see them. I've got to know...." Slowly she moved forward.

Watching her, Trevor nodded and then followed her into the darkness of the tunnel.

Zach held his breath. The soldiers were just a few feet from them on the road. With an inward sigh he eased from the concealment of the bramble and followed the woman and old man.

The two men were as Zach had left them, one on top of the other. Trevor gently rolled them apart.

Zach needed no confirmation of their death. While Trevor felt for a pulse on each, the young man climbed the bank and carefully peeked through the thorny blackberry bushes as the trucks and jeeps came back from the lake and turned down the narrow county road.

Trevor sighed. "They're dead." He stood silently for a moment. "But at least we know they aren't Caden or David."

Maria shook her head. "They were loved by someone."

Trevor nodded as his face grew tired and seemed to droop. He slumped to the bank beside the two bodies. After a few moments he said, "This place isn't safe. We need to head back to the house."

Maria closed her eyes and shook her head. "We can't leave them like this."

Zach slid down the bank and stopped beside the other two. "I think the soldiers are trying to get around the lake by using the logging road."

Trevor shook his head "They can't. We dug out the culvert and hid it."

"They've got a bulldozer," Zach said. "Could they make a temporary road across the stream?"

Trevor rubbed his chin and stared at the ground. "Maybe, but what can we do about it?"

The young man shrugged.

The older man turned toward the house. "Let's head home. After the fighting is over we'll tell Caden where to find these two— but I suspect he already knows."

Zach followed, but stopped abruptly. "The soldiers had a radio." He pointed to the bramble. "Could you use it to contact your people?"

Maria frantically searched for the device and found it before Trevor or Zach got there. She fumbled with it and then put it close to her lips. "Caden, hello or come in. Please Caden, come in."

From the radio came an anxious voice, "Maria? Is that you?"

"They shot two of your men near the farm. We came to help, but they're dead."

The radio crackled. "Get away from there!"

"I will but I've got to tell you—the convoy is heading down Hops Road. I think they're going to the logging road where the men removed the culvert."

There was a long pause. "Roger, thanks. Now, get away from there!"

Maria stepped toward the culvert with the radio, but Trevor stopped her. "If they catch us with military equipment they will shoot us as spies. Leave it here. If we're caught we can say we're just locals trying to get home."

She nodded and set the device beside the bodies.

The trip back to the farmhouse was uneventful and quiet. Zach heard only a single car pass on the road as they returned along the gully of the stream. Approaching the farm he saw Sheriff Hoover's car in front of the house. *What now?* He hung back as Trevor and Maria walked up to the officer. *Apparently this family has a better relationship with the police than mine.* Slowly he advanced until he

15

could hear the conversation.

"...don't believe it," the sheriff exclaimed, "They murdered two guardsmen?"

Trevor nodded. "They did."

"Nuclear terror attacks, looting, and chaos and now, just when I thought things might return to normal, American soldiers shoot their own countrymen. The world has turned upside down." Hoover shook his head. "Well they're out of town now. Most of them have headed down the county road. I don't know where they hope to go."

Trevor looked in the direction the convoy went. "Could they use the bulldozer to build a dam, maybe a temporary road, or maybe narrow the stream and use logs to build a short bridge?"

"I'm no engineer, but...maybe." The sheriff kicked a rock as he seemed to consider the idea. "We need to warn Caden."

"We did," Maria explained about the radio.

"I wonder if we could keep them from coming back." Trevor said. "Block the county road and the highway like we did before."

The sheriff smiled. "We couldn't do it as well as before, but we could make it difficult for them." Sitting in his patrol car he advised dispatch to secure two dump trucks. "Use one to block the highway at the narrow spot near the top of the hill and bring the other to the Westmore farm." He took a deep breath and then continued. "They killed two of the local guardsmen just west of town."

"Roger, Sheriff. The bodies of two other guardsmen were found east of the city limit along the highway."

Hoover sighed. "Notify the auxiliaries, the Legion, VFW and the guys who volunteered before. If they want to help, have them come to the Westmore farm. Out."

He hung the microphone back on the radio and, with furrowed brow, stood beside his car.

As the sound of gunfire echoed across the valley, they waited.

"I called Mom." Vicki walked up to Zach. "She wants us to stay put till the soldiers leave."

He nodded. "She makes sense—when she's sober."

Vicki walked off in a huff.

Using his binoculars, Trevor scanned the area. "I can't see any lookouts."

"Wouldn't they be hidden?" Maria said.

"Probably. They are trying to conceal their movements from Caden, but they haven't bothered hiding from us. I don't think they're concerned about the civilians—that's their mistake." Trevor pointed to the highway. "The dump truck is coming."

Zach looked in that direction. Police and other cars followed the truck.

The parade of vehicles rumbled up the dirt driveway to the Westmore home and formed an arch around part of the house and barn like the circling of wagons from a different era.

Soon a small crowd of people waited at the edge of the porch. Trevor moved to the top of the steps while Hoover stopped at the bottom.

Trevor told the assembled men about the two guardsmen that were killed along the highway. As he did he pointed to the spot in the distance. "Two more were shot east of town. They may be soldiers, but they no longer respect our laws, our traditions, or our Constitution. Furthermore, they are trying to kill those among us who are standing up for those principles. We want to keep these men out of our town, like we stopped the looters after the nuke attacks."

There was a murmur of agreement.

During the chaos of the terrorist attacks Zach's girlfriend, DeLynn, had suggested that he volunteer as a guard on the blockade, but his mother had called him a kid and said, "I won't have you messing with guns." So he watched and did nothing while others saved the community. *This time I won't ask her. DeLynn will be proud of me.*

Hoover nodded slowly and then walked up the steps. Standing beside Trevor on the porch he said, "Ben Franklin once said, 'We must all hang together or, we shall all hang separately.' Everyone needs to understand, once we engage the army there will be no turning back. Either we succeed, die trying, or die as traitors."

"We'll succeed, just like we did before," someone said.

Again, there was a murmur of agreement and the crowd dispersed toward the vehicles.

Zach walked with the flow. This time he was determined to be part of the action.

At the edge of the cars, an old man with a scraggily gray beard stood beside an ancient red pickup. "Do you have an extra gun?" Zach asked. "I'd like to help."

The old man looked at him with a skeptical eye. "How old are you?"

"Eighteen."

He rubbed his beard and looked at the boy doubtfully.

"I was going to enlist this summer." It was a lie, but Zach told it with all the conviction he could muster. He saw two military type guns in the cab and hoped that the man would not give him one as he had no idea how to use it.

The man reached behind the seat and grabbed a rifle. "Here," and handed it, and a box of ammo, to him.

Zach knew it was a hunting rifle, but knew nothing about the caliber or where the safety was located. "Thanks." He jumped in the back of the pickup. He slid down so no one, especially his sister, would see him.

Another man, about the same age, joined the first in the cab.

Zach examined the gun. It was a Remington .270 caliber, single-shot rifle. As the pickup pulled away from the farm and bumped along the dirt driveway he figured out how to load it.

All Zach could hear was the dump truck and other vehicles as the pavement ended and the convoy rumbled onto the dirt logging road. With each passing minute his heart beat harder in his chest. *The soldiers are going to kill us. Why did I want to come along?* The gun he had wanted just moments ago now felt heavy and foreign.

Over the rumble of engines came the sound of rapid gunfire. His stomach churned. He considered jumping from the back of the truck, but pride overruled fear.

He turned to look as the pickup slid to an abrupt stop on the gravel. Momentum threw Zach up against the cab. Metallic thuds and pings told him the pickup was taking fire.

The old man cursed and flew from the truck as glass rained down on Zach. The other man in the pickup was dead, his shattered, bloody head hung out the broken rear window.

Zach's eyes fixed on the crimson spectacle for several moments. Then he forced himself to peek over the edge. His muscles were stiff and unwilling to move like the time he fell into an icy pond.

"Come on boy. Better get to cover or...." The old man flew back and slammed to the ground. A blood stain grew on his chest.

Zach flung himself out of the truck and quickly scurried

along the ground toward a large tree. Once behind it he stared away from the battle frozen by fear.

He leaned hard against the rough bark as if somehow he could merge with it and disappear. *The two soldiers killed by the creek...the two men from the pickup...four people dead right in front of me—all in a few hours!* Then he realized the rifle he had been given was still in the truck. *How long before they find it and kill me?* Tears welled in his eyes. Images of DeLynn, her flowing blonde hair and deep blue eyes, flashed through his mind. *Will I ever see her...hold her...kiss her again?*

He forced himself to peek around the edge of the tree. The battle floated in his tears. About a dozen police and civilians formed a line along the cars and trucks as they fired down the hill.

Limbs fell from trees.

Dirt flew in the air.

Men fell.

Zach prayed.

Gradually the pace of fire slowed.

As the gunfire lulled, Zach wiped the tears from his face and ran forward, determined to retrieve the rifle. Fear made his feet swift and his body low to the ground. Nearing the pickup he scooped up a black military-style rifle. His momentum brought him to the truck with a thud.

His heart raced, but time seemed to crawl as Zach sat with his back against a rear tire of the truck. He examined the rifle. The receiver was open and no bullet was in the chamber. *Is there ammo in the magazine?* He pulled on it, but it didn't budge. The only thing he knew how to use was the scope, but he didn't want a close up view of the battle.

He wanted to do something, but didn't know what. Fear planted him where he was. Three yards away was the body of the old man who gave him the hunting rifle. *Why did I come?* He fumbled with the assault rifle. *I don't even know how to use this thing. What can I do?*

When only a few shots echoed along the narrow valley, Zach mustered his courage and stood just high enough to reach into the bed and retrieve the hunting rifle. He had already loaded it, but looking at his shaking hands he wasn't sure he could hit anything with it. He prayed the letup in gunfire signaled an end to the battle.

In the distance he heard someone shout, "Your position is hopeless. Throw down your weapons and you will not be harmed."

Several moments passed before he heard a woman shout, "We surrender."

Zach stood, wondering which side gave up.

"Pile your weapons in the road and line up along the shore," the voice in the distance commanded.

As several police and civilians moved toward the river, Zach followed. He slung the military rifle across his back and held the other in his hands. The men with him moved cautiously forward with rifles at the ready. *Did we win?*

As he reached the far side of the road he saw the soldiers piling their rifles and raising their hands in the air.

Tears of relief welled in Zach's eyes.

Those with him smiled and several patted him on the back, but he knew the truth. Again he had done nothing to help. He had hidden behind a tree crying and never fired a shot.

I am a coward.

CHAPTER FIVE

In a fog of despair, Caden helped load the wounded in the back of a deuce and a half and then in an ambulance that arrived on scene. When that was done he carried the body of Captain Turner to the back of a pickup. He stared at the body for a moment. "No, this isn't right."

"What?" Maria asked cautiously.

"A flag. He needs an American flag."

Maria ran off as Caden stared at the body.

A moment later she returned and handed him the flag he wanted.

Caden draped it over his fallen friend and tucked it under. When he was done, Maria held his hand and all but led him to the backseat of the cab. There the two sat silently together.

Turner wasn't the first friend to die in battle. Every time one of his men fell he questioned his decisions and tactics, but Turner wasn't one of his men. Caden's decisions and tactics had been sound and those good decisions cost Turner his life.

Friend against friend. Brother against brother. This hasn't happened since the Civil War.

Leading a convoy of the living and the dead, the driver pulled away from the battlefield at a solemn pace.

Is that what this is? The first battle of the next civil war? God, I pray that it isn't.

They passed a grove of alder trees. *So, barren...so dead.*

Maria squeezed his hand.

How many of our own people were killed or wounded? He would need a report from Brooks as soon as possible. *Letters need to be written…families consoled.*

He looked at Maria's hand, still clutching his, and then to her face. "You shouldn't have come."

"Why? I wanted to help."

As the truck rumbled along the driveway of the Westmore farm, he saw Hoover and Brooks talking on the porch. Along the side of the road a lone young man with red-hair walked with slumped shoulders. Slung across his back was an AR-15 and he carried a hunting rifle. As they passed, Caden realized he had often seen the lad fishing along the highway. *Did he fight in the battle?* Caden shook his head. *So young.*

The driver pulled to a stop. A red-haired girl ran toward the young man, but stopped several feet away. Tears left streaks along her face.

That young man is in big trouble.

Caden sighed and turned to Maria. "I've got to go. There could be more attacks. Wounded need to be checked on. Men redeployed."

Maria nodded. "I'll help with the wounded."

He kissed her and stepped from the cab. Taking a deep breath, he stood tall, assumed a more resolute countenance than he felt. Then he turned and marched toward Hoover and Brooks and the troubles ahead.

CHAPTER SIX

The sun was high, but Zach felt little of its warmth as he arrived back at the Westmore farm. The prisoners had been marched away, the wounded taken to the hospital. Zach was surrounded by the living. Many smiled. Some were solemn, but he was numb.

His sister ran toward him, but stopped abruptly about a yard away. Her eyes were wide and her face streaked with tears. When Vicki spoke her voice was tinged with anger. "I was scared when I couldn't find you. Even more frightened when I figured out you had gone to the battle." She paused as tears welled in her eyes. Her voice grew slow and sad. "Each body, every wounded man, I looked them all in the face hoping that each one wasn't you." She turned and walked toward home.

Zach followed. "I'm sorry Sis. I didn't think. I didn't mean…."

She turned and faced him, her voice shrill. "You're right. You didn't think." Tears came in a torrent. She ran ahead.

The weight of his foolish decisions pressed down on Zach. Going with the men had been a stupid decision. He was nothing more than a scared, moving target on the battlefield, and he had frightened Vicki.

She was yards away now, walking with anger-inspired speed.

Seeing Trevor he handed the hunting rifle to him. Trevor gave him a funny look, but Zach hurried after his sister.

They walked nearly a mile before Zach caught up with her. "I'm really sorry."

She wiped her face, and nodded. "What are you going to do with the gun?"

"The gun?" Zach looked down at the strap across his chest. He had been vaguely aware that the assault rifle was still on his back, but he hadn't thought about what to do with it. It belonged to the old guy from the pickup, but he was dead. Zach looked back in the direction of the Westmore farm, now hidden by trees, and then to his sister. "I don't know."

"Do you plan to keep it? Mom won't let you."

He shrugged and as they continued to walk he pondered the possibility. Vicki was right, their mother would never agree to keep a firearm in the house. "The world is going crazy and we need to protect ourselves. I'm not going to tell her about the gun."

"She'll see it."

"I'll hide it in the shed."

When they crossed the highway, the bodies of the two soldiers were gone. In silence they collected their traps and the fish within. Zach struggled to find a way to carry his share of the load with the rifle on his back. Satisfied he had distributed the weight of the fish and traps evenly, he continued along the stream with Vicki in the lead.

Climbing the hill toward home, Vicki asked, "Do you know how to shoot a gun?"

He held the rifle as if to shoot it and gazed through the scope with a confident air. "It's easier than the bow." He purposely avoided answering her question. "Don't tell Mom I went to the battle. It'll just make her mad."

"Yeah, it would. Dad got killed and now you decide to be a war hero."

The word hero brought the fear and panic of hours ago back to mind. He felt his face flush. His eyes drifted toward the ground.

Vicki shook her head. "I won't tell her."

As they approached the trailer Zach said, "Go on in. I'll be along in a moment." He made a wide arc so as to remain hidden by the trees and brush. Stepping out of the woods near the shed he sprinted to the door. Once inside he dropped the traps near the entrance. His bow and quiver hung from the wall near the back and that was where he went next. Moving boxes aside, he leaned the rifle into the corner and re-stacked the cartons around it.

Carrying only his portion of the daily catch, he walked in the front door of the trailer.

*   *   *

Caden wondered if it was some form of cognitive dissonance. The Battle of Olympia, of which the Hansen skirmish was a small part, was just days passed. Many had died, including his friend Turner. But today, for the first time since the battle, he was smiling. Beside Maria's bed, he had left a tray with a cup of coffee, a ring, and a note. The band was an old one, his grandmother's, but it was all he had. When she came down, Maria wore it. "Yes," she said and kissed him.

Driving into Hansen, still lost in the glow of the morning memories, Caden noticed the two red-haired teens only as he passed them. They were placing fish traps in the stream near the highway. Impulsively he decided to stop and talk to them. Out of habit he looked in his mirrors, but his was the only car on the road. He considered stopping in the lane, but chose to pull to the shoulder.

He stepped from the car and waved. The two youths set the traps aside and walked toward the road. In normal times, fish traps were illegal, but these were not normal times and no one seemed interested in bothering people as they attempted to feed themselves.

Caden walked back along the highway. Remembering the ceremony later in the day, he tried not to get mud on his shoes and uniform as he started down the bank.

The three met near the bottom.

The young girl's eyes seemed fixed on the military issue holster and pistol on Caden's hip. The boy followed his sister's gaze, but quickly locked on Caden's eyes.

"My family told me about your help earlier in the week before and during the battle. That you told them about the soldiers that were shot..."

Zach looked off to the side.

"...and led them back to where it happened."

"Yeah, it was right over there. It feels strange being here now, so near the spot, but we have to eat and this is a good location for the traps."

Caden looked at Zach, but the boy averted his eyes. "You're brave," he gestured toward the fish traps, "and more resourceful than most."

25

Zach shook his head, but said nothing as his gaze slumped to the ground.

He sensed that Zach wanted to say more, but the boy remained silent staring at the earth. "Anyway, thank you for your help." He climbed the bank to his car and drove toward town.

His first stop that morning was the sheriff's office. As Caden walked in, Hoover sat on the edge of his desk staring at pages held in his hand. At the edge of his vision, Caden detected movement and turned. Dr. Scott looked up from a collection of papers on a table before her.

Caden wasn't sure how long she had been a doctor in the community but, from his perspective, she had always been there, always been a doctor and always had gray hair. However, it was unusual to see the law-abiding doctor in the sheriff's office so, he asked, "What brings you here?"

"Pestilence—unfortunately."

"What?"

The doctor sighed and leaned back in her chair. "There's a new strain of influenza with a high mortality rate spreading in FEMA camps around what is left of L.A. and San Diego."

"Southern California is a long way off." Caden shrugged.

"Yes, but flu has a habit of spreading."

"Is there a shot for this type?"

She shrugged. "This strain is so new we don't know how effective the current vaccine will be." Her eyes drifted to the floor. "I should have tried to get more flu serum, but there are so many meds we need, so many shortages."

"As I remember flu hits the young and old really hard." Caden recalled the last time he'd seen Hoover's mother in the hospital. He wanted to ask how she was doing, but this didn't seem like the time.

"The very old, those with serious medical conditions, the particularly vulnerable, most of them are already dead."

Caden glanced at the sheriff. *Nope, not a good time to ask about your mother.* "What do you think we should do?"

"That was what we were discussing," Hoover said. "We can't block off the town again. Some food and medicine is coming in and the mayor and county commissioners are trying to get the economy up and running again."

Scott nodded. "Dr. Winfield went to the Longview camp yesterday...."

"Who?" Caden asked.

"Winfield from the camp that was just outside of town on the North Road. He agreed to stay on at our hospital and has been a great help. Anyway he told me that there are over a quarter of a million people in and around the site. They're doing their best, but it's a breeding ground for infection. Dysentery and typhoid are constant dangers."

Even the best of the camps Caden had seen were to be avoided. In every camp the mixture of decay, body odor and human waste hung heavy in the air like some toxic cologne of the Devil. Disease was always a worry. Caden shuddered involuntarily.

"We have checkpoints on the roads coming into town," Caden said. "What if we train the men to look for symptoms? If they show signs they don't get in."

"They could still be carriers without showing signs." The doctor shrugged. "But, without an effective vaccine for this strain, that may be the best we can do."

Hoover nodded and walked over to a large map of the county. "The combination of Guard checkpoints and police patrols keeps the state highway safe from the mountain pass in the east to the freeway in the west. The North Road is clear to Olympia. Our weak area is to the south. That's what I want to talk to you about." He looked at Caden. "Farms and homes are being raided south of here." Hoover pointed to several small towns. "Bandits have put up roadblocks to rob travelers." He pointed to spots along several highways. "I need your help restoring law and order, and securing the roads."

"With the war preparations we're stretched thin, but I'll see what we can do," Caden said.

Hoover shook his head. "I guess the terrorists won. People are hungry, scared and fighting each other."

"They won the first battle, but if the terrorists ultimately defeat us it will be because Durant assumed dictatorial powers and cut a deal with the Chinese."

Hoover remained silent.

"Are you having second thoughts?" Caden asked.

"I was angry the day of the battle. I wanted to stop the

soldiers who shot our people. But now I wonder if we can't find a better way."

"If Durant allows the presidential election, removes restrictions on the press, and recognizes the new congress, I'm sure there won't be a war."

"That's not going to happen."

Caden shrugged. "Then the country will continue to split and the economy collapse."

The doctor stood. "You two can talk about politics, I've got patients to take care of."

Hoover nodded and the doctor turned and departed.

Hoover returned his attention to Caden. "The economy is collapsing—there's food in the grocery store around the corner, but have you seen the prices?"

Caden shook his head.

"It costs over five dollars for a can of corn or green beans. Trucks are moving, commerce should be getting back to normal, but no one trusts the money. Most say it's worthless and won't accept it as payment. Inflation is…well, out of control."

"My dad never had much faith in paper money. I guess a lot of people agree with him now. We may not be able to change the current situation but, hopefully, most people were prepared for it and can endure until life gets better."

"Aren't you the philosopher." Hoover grinned.

Caden smiled. "I'll let you know if we can get patrols for those communities in the south." He turned to leave and then stopped. "There was a red-haired teen at the battle with us. His first name is Zach…."

"Zachary Brennon. Yeah what about him?"

"No one in my family knew him. I guess I'm just curious. It's remarkable that one so young would help in such deadly serious actions."

"He's a minor, but not all that young." Hoover turned to his computer and typed with two fingers. When the file appeared, he nodded. "Sixteen. He's been arrested four times."

"Really?" Caden's eyes widened. "He didn't seem like a bad kid."

Hoover shrugged as he looked at the file. "Misguided. Dad was killed ten, maybe eleven, years ago."

"Do you know what happened?"

"I remember some. It was a robbery." Again, the sheriff typed with his index fingers. He leaned closer to the screen and put on his glasses. "At the time the family owned the convenience store beside the freeway, the one across from the church."

Images flashed through Caden's mind of Henry, the farmer from Oregon, camped in the parking lot and the reunion with his father on the night of the gunfight across the street at the church. "Yeah," he said, "I know the place."

"A three-time loser crackhead entered demanding money. The Dad had a bat, crackhead had a gun." The sheriff shrugged. "We arrested the perp the next day. He was so high he didn't even try to run."

"So, the boy needs a father figure...some direction?"

"Maybe. Mom is a drunk." He looked back at the computer screen. "Zach's first arrest was when he was nine years old. He shoplifted shoes. Later that year, on Christmas Eve, he was arrested when he tried to shoplift a dollhouse from a toy store on Main Street." Hoover laughed. "The kid may have more issues than I thought." His eyes seemed to look far away. "I remember that store. The old guy made the dollhouses, rocking horses, cars and trucks himself—out of wood." He shook his head. "Nobody does work like that anymore."

"Anyway, about Zach, you think he's just misguided?" Caden shrugged. "Maybe he needs some direction."

"I'd advise you to stay away. If you haven't noticed, the world is falling apart. Like we were talking about, the money is near worthless, the stores are almost empty and I'm sure you haven't forgotten that we started a civil war last week. I don't have time to play daddy to a neglected kid."

"No, neither do I...but...."

CHAPTER SEVEN

Caden looked left as he stepped from the sheriff's office. Up the next street, beyond the county office building, he saw part of the grocery store parking lot. He didn't often drive that way, but his conversation with Hoover made him want to see what was happening. Glancing at his watch he decided he had time to visit the shop, and set out on foot across the deserted intersection.

The establishment had started as a local grocery, but it had been sold and remodeled several times over the years. It was now the largest food store in town.

The last time he drove past the market it had been closed, and the glass broken out. Grocery stores were early targets for looters, even one this close to the sheriff's office.

A dozen cars dotted the lot, and most appeared to be makeshift homes. As Caden walked diagonally across, teenagers played soccer in a corner of the nearly empty expanse of asphalt. *There's a park a block away. Why don't they play there?*

The store had more plywood than glass in the windows and doors. As he approached, he still wasn't sure the place was open. Tacked to the plywood were signs in bold print, "No checks or credit." Underneath someone had written, "Cash, gold or silver only."

The automatic doors hadn't budged and Caden was about to walk away when the sound of a motor drew his attention to a security camera above and to his left. He stared into the lens for a moment and then the doors lumbered open.

Just inside a man with thin gray-hair sat in the corner against the wall on a green plastic lawn chair. A pump shotgun rested on his lap, and he held a jury-rigged switch connected to the door by wires. A nearby TV displayed the outside view of the door, switched to the parking lot and then back.

The eyes of the guard seemed to be on Caden's butt as he passed. The thought was disconcerting, however he quickly realized it was not his shapely backside the guard eyed, but the holster on his hip. Then their eyes met and the guard nodded.

Caden's eyes lingered on the shotgun for a moment. *That's one way to stop theft.*

The coffee shop at the front was closed. A young cashier hovered around the only store register in use. The others were blocked off with boxes and carts. Caden continued down a thinly-stocked produce aisle. Potatoes, peas and iceberg lettuce were available and a few things he didn't recognize. He walked past one item that looked like peas, but the sign read "Edamame." Another looked like onions, but was turnips. Farther along, the canned goods aisle appeared full, but on closer inspection the cans had been pulled forward. The illusion of plenty was a thin façade. Where normally there would be forty or fifty of an item there was now a facing of ten.

Caden searched out the items the sheriff had mentioned. He found the green beans first. *Hoover was wrong; they only cost $4.99 a can.* He shook his head. *Maybe 'only' isn't the right word to use.* Next he came to the corn and sighed. It was $5.29 a can.

Shaking his head, Caden turned the corner on the next aisle. He had passed fewer than ten people since entering the store and two of them were employees. A woman pushed a cart with a dozen items toward the register. Just behind her was a man. *A bored husband, a bodyguard, or both.*

He anticipated an empty meat counter, but when it came in view he saw beef, pork, chicken, and local varieties of fish. *The beef and pork are probably from the nearby packing plant. Does Zach supply the fish?* He wondered if all the fresh food was local. It seemed likely during the current chaos and upheaval. Signs along the top of the meat counter declared "Ask for prices." So he did.

"What are you interested in?" The butcher inquired.

"That." He pointed to a whole chicken.

"Nine dollars a pound." The man lifted it from the display.

For chicken? "Thanks, but not today." *What does a steak go for? No, I don't want to know.* Walking away he shook his head. *I've gained a new respect for livestock on the farm.*

He continued along the back toward the far wall where he saw a small, in store, branch bank. A man with salt-and-pepper hair counted out a large stack of bills for an older woman.

When she walked away, stuffing the money in her purse, the banker looked at Caden, "Can I help you?"

Caden shook his head and then reconsidered. After introducing himself he added, "I'm checking prices and trying to understand how the local economy is functioning."

The man scowled. "Not well. The woman who was at the counter when you walked up…she's fairly well situated, but she's withdrawing savings to buy a few days of food. What happens when her savings run out?"

Caden nodded. "Hopefully we can get enough aid to hold us over until more can be grown locally."

"If we don't…." He was silent for a moment. "As far as I can tell no one received Social Security payments this month. Those checks were meager to begin with. Now…."

He shook his head. "If inflation continues at the current rate many of the elderly will soon be homeless and hungry even if Social Security resumes payments."

Under the current circumstances Caden couldn't imagine Hoover evicting little old ladies, but in other places it probably would happen. He looked around, but didn't see a single customer. "You would think more people would be buying all the food they could."

"Most people don't have the cash to buy here. The place with the most economic activity is the market in Library Park."

"Yes, I've been there." *And I'll go there when I leave here.*

The banker continued. "In the past wealth was how many dollars you had, but it doesn't take much to destroy confidence in a currency. During the terrorist attacks people quickly learned that all the cash they had couldn't buy them the gas or food they needed. Those things disappeared from store shelves, and the owners were stuck with paper money, but nothing to eat.

"Since the attacks people spend their dollars quickly for useful or practical things they may need or to use in trade. They still save, but now it's tangible items or gold and silver, not paper money.

That lack of confidence and need for real wealth is being seen as inflation." The banker shook his head. "I've read about it in the history books and seen it in third world countries, but I never thought I'd see a currency collapse in the United States."

"If the value of paper money has collapsed, why does the store still accept it?"

"As it says on all bills, 'This note is legal tender for all debts, public and private.' The store pays its taxes, lease, electric bill and employees with checks drawn on cash. The bank pays the sublease to the store with a check backed by cash. But everyone is trying to unload the dollars as fast as possible because they are losing value daily."

As he walked toward the exit, the older woman stood at the checkout handing over a wad of bills for two bags of groceries. He had no solution for her or the growing number of hungry people and that realization felt like a huge weight pressing down on him.

Caden nodded to the guard at the door and the old man shifted the gun to one side and flipped the switch. The doors creaked and groaned open. As Caden walked from the store, he realized the soccer game had paused.

The teens eyed him carefully.

Caden rested his hand on the holster and stared at the boys for a moment. Then with his eyes forward, but using his peripheral vision to watch them, he walked across the parking lot and on toward his car.

His thoughts had already turned to his upcoming wedding when he heard the scream. He turned around, but could see only a slice of the store parking lot.

Caden ran three steps toward the store when the boom of shotgun filled the air.

He pulled his pistol and ran faster.

Now he could see the teens running with the old lady's grocery bags. One was torn spilling cans, but the boys that followed quickly scooped them up and sprinted away behind the others.

The guard stood in the entryway of the store sweeping his shotgun from side to side.

The woman leaned against a car with one hand on her chest.

Caden and the guard reached her at about the same moment. Both asked if she was okay.

Still leaning on the car and looking down, she didn't answer.

"I shot over their heads. Perhaps I should have aimed lower," the guard growled.

Caden, his eyes fixed on the woman, didn't answer. "Are you okay?"

Hand still clutching her chest, she stared at him with wide frightened eyes. Then she fell to the pavement.

CHAPTER EIGHT

Bent in half with one arm twisted underneath and the other out to the side, the elderly woman lay motionless.

"Call 911!" Caden ordered as he knelt beside her. He gently shook her. "Are you all right?" *Stupid question.* He laid her flat, checked for breathing and a pulse, but found neither and began CPR.

Movement caught Caden's eye. A deputy ran toward them speaking into his shoulder radio. The officer took over breathing while Caden performed chest compressions.

Several minutes ticked by in surreal slow motion. By the time the wail of a siren was heard drops of sweat rolled down Caden's face and dripped on the old woman's blouse.

When the EMTs arrived, Caden stood and backed away. As he did, he saw Hoover trotting across the parking lot.

Reaching Caden the sheriff said, "The deputy reported Judge Hastings was down. What happened?"

"She's a judge?

"Yes, she was…."

"She was mugged,"

Hoover shook his head. "I'll need a statement from you."

"And then I think she had a heart attack."

The sheriff's expression slowly changed from sadness to anger. "She was the chief judge until she retired a few years ago…"

The EMTs lifted the body onto a gurney. There were no more attempts to revive her.

"…and she was my friend."

*   *   *

Caden's trip to the Library Park market was delayed until Monday, but even then he was thinking about the death of Judge Hastings. *Conditions in the FEMA camps are worse than here in Hansen. If kids attack people for food here, what is happening in the camps? And will it spread to here?*

The number of sellers had grown, taking over a used car lot across the street. The mixture of music, smoke, colorful tarps and rough wood stalls gave the place a third-world bazaar look. The music seemed to be live, but he couldn't see the band as he entered the winding lanes covering the park.

Immediately on his left was a large community bulletin board with a second, new board, beside it. In the center of one was a notice of food aid distribution from the Salvation Army. Sprinkled around it were announcements of church services, a public meeting at Legion Hall, and another told of school opening, but asked students to bring lunch until further notice. On his first trip to the market he had seen a poster pleading for insulin. He didn't see it this time and wondered if the supply was better or the diabetics had died.

Farther in the maze stalls sold everything that could be grown during a western Washington winter including spinach, cauliflower and, he read the sign, kale. Stacks of commercial and home canned food items stood at the next stall. Chickens in cages cackled next to baskets full of eggs at the next. Beyond that a man sold firewood.

He was staring at jars of honey when he felt something pull at his holster. Instinctively, he turned and grabbed at the puller. Just for a moment he held the snout of a goat on a long tether.

The animal jerked backwards uttering a loud, "baaa."

Caden shook his head and walked away. Several minutes later, the goat nibble all but forgotten, his thoughts turned to the vibrancy of this market compared to the emptiness of the grocery store. Dollars changed hands in both and prices were as exorbitant here as the store. However, barter and trade were common in Library Park and ammunition served as an alternate currency.

In the distance, he spotted a sign reading, "Gold and Silver Exchange." Nearing the stall he saw a middle-aged man behind the counter buying precious metals for large bundles of paper money.

As he watched, several people brought rings, necklaces, and other jewelry in exchange for cash. Caden assumed they were using it in the market or nearby stores to buy food and other necessities. He grinned. *This guy is acting as a bank for the market.*

Catching a glimpse of something hanging from the man's belt, Caden stepped across the lane to a food stall. With the change of angle he saw a pistol and holster on the old man's hip. Caden grinned knowingly. *Of course he would be armed.*

Scanning the crowd, Caden also spotted a nearby deputy chatting with a young woman.

"You want anything?"

He turned toward the voice. "What?"

The woman behind the counter smiled, "You've been standing at my counter. I wondered if you wanted anything."

He looked at several bundles of a leafy plant he recognized, but couldn't name. "What is this?"

"Chard or Swiss Chard. I've been growing it for years. It's a very nutritious vegetable."

He listened as the woman extolled the history and virtues of various plants and was almost convinced to buy when he realized he had no money.

As Caden walked on he noticed two Hispanic men, ten yards away, watching him. They turned when he spotted them, and whispered to each other. Then they moved several yards farther down the walkway, but still glanced at both the money changer and Caden. After a moment they spoke to each other and left.

They appeared to be casing the stall, but they'd be crazy to try and rob the old man with so many people around. Still, why were they looking at me? He remembered he was in uniform with a pistol on his belt. *That's plenty of reason to watch me. They were probably just looking like I was. Heck, I even changed position to get a good view of his pistol.* Caden shook his head. *I'm being paranoid and maybe a bit racist.*

Caden continued in another direction until he spotted Zach about twenty yards ahead, talking to a pretty blonde girl about his age. Her jeans and jacket were nicer than the casual attire of most at the market.

On the ground by Zach was a white bucket from which he retrieved a large trout. The girl held out a plastic container and Zach slid in the fish. She kissed him on the cheek and hurried away. The boy watched, until she disappeared around a bend, then he lifted the bucket and walked slowly with his head down, toward Caden.

As Zach approached, Caden asked, "Is she a friend of yours?"

Startled, the boy's head shot up. "Oh, hi…ah, yeah…just a girl from school." His face grew redder with each word.

Caden turned and walked with the boy. "I thought you would be fishing."

Zach shook his head. "After we set the traps we leave them and I come here to help."

Ahead Zach's sister stood at a stall. A red-haired woman worked beside her. Behind them, sitting in a lawn chair, was a potbellied man with black hair, and a flashy Hawaiian-style shirt. He wondered if the mom had remarried or if the man was just a friend. *Perhaps there is a man that can provide some guidance and direction for Zach.* Glancing at his watch he asked, "Isn't the school open?"

The young man grinned. "Yeah, but right now eating is more important."

Caden wondered what his mother thought of that plan. He pointed and asked, "Is that your mom and dad?"

The boy's face darkened. "Yeah that's my mom, but he's not my father. His name is Bo. Dad had red hair, like my mom…like Vicki." And then almost in a whisper he added, "Like me."

Zach did not elaborate and Caden still didn't know what role Bo filled in the family, but decided not to ask. He said goodbye and turned back the way he came.

As he left the market he still wanted to help Zach, but didn't know how. He wanted to help the community, but he had no answers to the vexing problems of the town. He stopped and looked back. This was the one place in town that had the hustle and bustle that was common before the attacks. Their resourcefulness gave him hope.

*   *   *

At the end of a long day, Caden entered the armory conference room with the duty roster in one hand and the Governor's Martial law edict in the other. On the large center table was a copy of the Seattle Times. It was the first newspaper he had seen since returning to the state. The headline shouted Hunger in Metro Area. Setting down what had been important, he picked up the Times. The lead story detailed food shortages in Tacoma and the fringes of the Seattle red zone. Also above the fold was the announcement that they were now publishing from temporary offices in Olympia. He glanced over articles about riots and looting. *I guess this is the new normal.*

When Brooks walked in, Caden paused his reading. "I forgot to mention yesterday that the sheriff wants help patrolling the towns south of Hansen."

Brooks walked over to a map of southwest Washington on the wall.

On page five of the six-page paper was a small article that quoted an Oregon investment banker: "The Chinese government had been selling dollars for a week before the first terror attack and dumped two trillion in United States treasury bonds on the market the morning of the Washington D.C. attack."

He was no economist, but Caden was sure that such an act would crush the value of the dollar. If the report was true, China knew of the attacks before they occurred, and perhaps planned them, and Durant had to know at least that much.

"We have one patrol south of town, but I don't see how we can send more," Brooks said. "We're already covering over 2,000 square miles. The Tacoma police want us to move our checkpoint on North Road closer to them and now Hoover wants us to patrol farther south? We're stretched beyond thin."

Setting the paper down, Caden looked at the map. "We need more people."

"The army could help?"

He shook his head. "Not unless President Durant decides to restore the Constitution. Every unit at the Joint Base will soon be heading east." Thinking about what would happen when those soldiers met units loyal to Durant caused him to shudder.

"If we had money we could recruit people."

"We have money, it's just not worth much, but we also have food and a warm place to sleep." He looked squarely at Brooks. "Start signing people up."

The XO sighed. "I guess we could recruit from the FEMA camps. They can't be feeding them all that well."

Caden thought for a moment. Getting people, even just a few, out of the camps before conditions got worse, was a good idea. "Go ahead, but recruit locals first and then people from the camp." He picked up his coffee cup from the table and drank the last of the lukewarm brew. Stepping to the side of his desk, he looked at the dark window reflecting his image. "What time is it?"

"18:30."

He dropped the papers. "I'm going home before Maria hunts me down. We're supposed to go over wedding plans tonight."

"I'll see you at dinner."

"What?"

"Lisa said your parents want to get to know me better. They invited me over."

Caden laughed. "Be afraid, be very afraid."

"Of your parents?"

Stepping through the door he said, "Of my little sister. She has plans for you." As he walked down the hall his phone rang. *Maria is hunting for me.* Then he looked at the caller ID. *The sheriff?* Quickly he answered the phone.

"Caden, there's been an attack."

CHAPTER NINE

At the end of another bone chilling day of fishing, Zach walked up the hill still smiling after his rendezvous with DeLynn. It had been brief, just dropping off a few fish so she and her parents, wouldn't go hungry. She had smiled and they exchanged a quick kiss. That was enough to give him hope for another day.

The moon peeked from behind the nearly solid cloud cover, casting a dim glow on his destination, the shed behind his home. Inside, he stowed the traps beside the net he was making. He stared toward the back where the rifle remained, but did not retrieve it. *Why did I take something I don't know how to use? I'm such an idiot.*

Intermittent flakes of snow greeted him as he stepped from the shed. Distant gunfire echoed in the hills. He paused and listened until he was certain it was far away. Then he continued to the dingy, single-wide trailer he called home.

Vicki, standing at the counter, sang to music only she could hear from the white earbuds that hung from her ears. With a knife in one hand she filleted, swayed and sang all at the same time.

Seeing him, she popped one bud out and opened the knife drawer. "I didn't hear you come in. She passed him a knife. "Did you give fish to DeLynn?"

He felt his face warm. "I gave a couple to her. How did you know?"

She grinned. "I didn't, but I know how many we catch and that we usually fillet a few less. I know it takes you forever to come in at night and I've seen how you look at her."

Again his face flushed. "Her parents don't want me around."

She smiled at him. "That's okay, big brother. They don't know you."

For the next few minutes they worked in silence. When a car drove up the winding driveway, Vicki went to the window. "Bo," she said with obvious disgust.

Bo and their mother stumbled into the house laughing. Both clutched bottles.

"Where did you get the booze?" Zach asked.

"A new business venture." Bo collapsed in a seat. He wore a suit with a red tie. "This is home brew. I buy it from the maker, drink some, share some with friends like Carol," he looked at Zach's mom, "and sell most of it."

Clumsily, his mom clutched two glasses and stumbled into a chair beside Bo.

Anger welled up in Zach like venom in a snake. He considered retrieving his new gun and chasing Bo off or, better yet, killing him, but he wasn't sure the rifle was even loaded or how to reload it if it wasn't.

As the two continued to sip the booze, Zach turned, retrieved a fish from the bucket and started gutting and filleting. *Why do you drink so much?* He didn't have words for the emotions of rejection, disappointment and fear that flooded him. *Why did Dad have to die?*

Zach stared at Bo. *You're the reason Mom is a drunk. I will kill you someday.* He grabbed another fish and with a savage thrust cut deep into its belly.

*   *   *

The sheriff's statement confused Caden. "An attack? What do you mean?"

"A gang broke into a home, killed a mother and child, and then killed the husband when he came home from the Library Park market and…"

Caden thought of the men he saw casing the money changer's stall.

"…then stole his gray Ford van."

With all the money, jewelry and precious metals in it. "Any more casualties?"

"One deputy was wounded and is in route to the hospital and they've shot at several civilians that got in the way during the chase. They're now in two vehicles, the van and a blue, older model Chevy lowrider. We believe the group is headed out of town…."

"What do you mean 'believe'? Aren't you following them?"

"We lost them when the deputy was shot…"

"Oh, sorry."

"…but based on the direction they were headed and the roads we've already blocked they'll pass your men either on the North Road or the main highway heading west."

"I'll alert my soldiers." Caden walked back toward the armory office and met Brooks at the door. "Dinner will be late tonight." He briefed the XO. "Give Fletcher a description of the autos and have him alert the sentries and patrol."

While Brooks talked with Fletcher on the phone, Caden stared at the county map on the wall. "I want you to take second squad and set up a position on the east side of the causeway. Maybe we can trap them on it. I'll take third squad and set up near the Cowlitz Bridge.

Hearing Brooks talk to Lisa over the phone, Caden pulled out his own. When Maria answered he said, "I may be late to dinner tonight."

*   *   *

Caden looked at his watch. He had been standing at the checkpoint on the north side of the Cowlitz River for nearly an hour. Sandbags formed a four-foot 'U' shaped wall about him. Two deuce and a half trucks formed a chokepoint at the edge of the bridge beside him. Drivers could pass through, but they had to go really slow.

He stomped his feet in the snow both to get the blood flowing and to relieve the boredom. As he turned to get another cup of coffee, the radio on his belt crackled.

"Caden, this is Hoover. I'm coming up on your position with lights flashing. Please don't shoot me."

He smiled and passed word to the men just as the lights of the squad car pierced the darkness.

After Hoover parked and walked up, Caden briefed him. "Nothing is happening."

Slowly the sheriff looked around and then, with a nod said, "Yeah, I can see that."

"The deputy that got shot, how is he?"

"Dr. Scott is working on him. We'll know more in the morning."

Caden then asked, "Who did the gang kill?"

"His name was Simon Pettit. He did ammo reloading in the market place."

"I figured it was the money changer."

"Nope. It was Simon."

For nearly a minute the two men looked down the road into the darkness and swirling snow.

"Did they get by us?" Caden asked.

Hoover shrugged. "Your perimeter checkpoints didn't spot them. I think they just stopped somewhere. They're waiting for things to cool." He stared ahead. "Or for us to make a wrong move. If I were them, I'd find some house on a side road, set back a way in the trees, bust in quick...." He let the sentence die.

Caden didn't want to imagine what would happen next but, as silence passed between them, he did.

Hoover stared into the darkness and then turned to Caden. "I'm going hunting. You be careful."

"Me be careful? I'm just waiting here, you're the one hunting for killers. Stop for a second."

Hoover paused. "What?"

Caden hollered to Fletcher, "You're in charge. Call me if anything happens." He then pointed at two soldiers, "You guys are with me."

As the men packed into a squad car, Hoover called over his shoulder radio for one of the deputies to meet him. Together they headed into the night in search of killers.

For over an hour they cautiously visited homes north and east of Hansen. As they left yet another one, Caden said, "The closer we get to my place the more nervous I'm getting."

Hoover smiled. "From what you've told me about Maria and what I know about your dad, they'd be fools to go near your place. Besides, they would call if anything happened."

Caden knew that was true. Still he thought about the Westmore farmhouse. It was off the main road, at the end of a long dirt driveway, trees blocked the view from many angles. However, it was on a hill and visible from numerous locations, not as secluded and surrounded by trees as the homes they had been checking. Still, he was concerned. *What if they see it and decide that is where they want to hide out?*

"Your turn Mr. Military."

"What?"

"To check out the place. A retired couple live here. The driveway is about a quarter of a mile long. You can't even see the house from here."

As the others set up a perimeter at the road edge, Caden walked toward the home. Approaching the dwelling was a problem. He didn't want to look like a criminal casing the place, but he didn't want to expose himself either. It seemed best to approach a residence unseen and check it out. Look for an illuminated room with curtains pulled back, observe, then knock and talk for final confirmation that all was well. However, this house was completely dark. *Probably no one is home. But what is open this late at night that an old....*

Booms and flashes tore from the house.

Caden dove into the snow.

In the darkness he heard movement and shots zinging past. He crawled with all his might for the nearby trees as headlights lit the driveway and the roar of engines filled the night air.

As the cars sped by, Caden shouted into his radio. "They're coming your way!"

The gunfire became continuous.

Staying low, Caden hurried through the trees as shots blasted back and forth along the driveway. The sound of crunching metal and breaking glass came from up ahead. He quickened his pace, but could only go so fast in the near total darkness of the forest. Approaching the road, Caden stopped. The van was not in sight, but the lowrider had hit a tree. Behind the vehicle were two people, one man was shooting at the soldiers and Hoover, the other was limp on the ground.

Taking careful aim at the torso, Caden fired a three round burst. The man dropped in a heap.

Within seconds the shooting died down.

"Hold your fire! It's me, Caden." He waved as he came out of the woods.

"Glad to see you're still with us," the sheriff said.

Caden trotted across the road to the lowrider and checked the first body. Three shots were in a tight group to the chest. The next man had been hit in both the head and chest. His mother couldn't have identified him.

Standing in the middle of the road Hoover asked, "Are they dead?"

"Yes."

"Come on then, we've got to follow that van." Hoover left the deputy at the house and called over the radio for backup at that location.

Caden was certain that the deputies would find all the gang members gone and no one alive in the house.

Hoover spun the tires of the squad car in the snow and then with a jolt regained traction. Caden called over his radio for third squad to come in their direction as they gathered speed and pursued the van.

*   *   *

A gunshot boomed nearby. Startled, Zach dropped his knife on the counter. Abandoning the last fish he had to fillet he tentatively stepped to the window and pulled the curtain back an inch or two.

More shots and muzzle flashes came from the road down the hill. *That's the direction of DeLynn's house.*

Zach looked at his mother asleep in the chair with a half-full glass of booze still in her hand.

Bo tried to stand, but fell awkwardly back in the chair. "Get away from the window boy, it's dangerous. Best to stay here with your mom and me."

Vicki never agreed with Bo, but this time she nodded with a worried look.

With a shake of the head the young man strode toward the door, grabbed his coat and stepped into the storm.

Despite the swirling wind and bang of gunfire, Zach heard shouts in Spanish. Curious but scared, he retrieved his bow from the shed. The military rifle might have been a more effective weapon, but he didn't know how to use it and was much more confident with the bow.

Out of hunting habit, Zach headed into the forest downwind of the noise. Making a large arch through woods he knew well, he slowly came back toward the clamor. It was clear the gunfight was along the road, but he could discern little else. Concerned that he might be hit by a stray bullet, he hiked back up the hill a few yards and moved parallel to the fight. Between the trees he snatched glimpses of a battle between soldiers and civilians.

Zach moved into a better position near the top of a steep slope. He strained to see detail. Only a single light from DeLynn's home and the glow of moonlight, diffused through clouds, provided illumination. From the tracks in the snow, it appeared the gray van had spun out in a turn and slid off the road. The occupants were using the vehicle as cover and firing on the advancing soldiers. From shouts in Spanish, Zach guessed that the civilians were members of a Mexican gang.

He was relieved that the fighting was not at DeLynn house, but it was close. Despite the fear that churned in his gut, he determined to stay nearby. He was surprised at his determination and relative calm. Perhaps it was because no one knew he was there and that he could hunker down and observe without being judged.

Behind the van the ground was steep and covered in wet snow. The gang hid behind the vehicle, but had no easy route of escape and the soldiers outnumbered them. Using the gully and woods along the road, the military cautiously advanced and, as they did, they gained greater angle of fire.

Zach spotted Caden with Sheriff Hoover and several men in the gully below him. Staying low, three of the men ran down the slope to a cluster of trees near the edge of the road. From there Zach caught a glimpse as they entered the forest. The young man knelt down behind a bush as the soldiers hurried past his position. It was soon clear these three were moving to a location where they could overlook the gang. Zach crawled to a good spot behind a large stump, ready to watch the unfolding battle as the soldiers on the hill with him opened fire.

Two of the gang fell immediately. Three others fled up the steep slope, falling to their hands and knees as they ran in a panic for the cover of the trees.

Movement near the van caught Zach's attention, but whatever it was quickly disappeared into darkness.

* * *

Hoover was beyond the vehicle on his way into the woods.

Caden called out to his men, "Stay close to them, but don't be heroic. They're hurt, probably low on ammo and cold. We can afford to wait for reinforcements before moving in."

With that, Staff Sergeant Fletcher led the squad into the forest leaving Caden and one soldier behind to examine the van and bodies.

"What's the ETA on second squad," Caden called over the radio.

"We're a couple of miles away…be there in two minutes," Brooks replied.

The private pointed to the van. A small fire flickered inside. "Should I check it out?"

Gun in hand, Caden stepped closer to the soldier and glanced at the name tag.

"Sure, Private Collins, let's check it out" With the young man a step ahead they approached the van.

A thunderous boom filled the air.

Caden gasped as he hit the snowy pavement hard. He tried to stand, but couldn't. Something was on his legs. Heat, like an oven, radiated from flames a few feet away. It was hard to see, harder to think. Caden pushed the smoldering bulk on his legs. It was soft.

The solder with me? "Private, are you okay?" When Caden nudged him again he felt something wet and warm. "If you can, I need you to…."

Movement at the edge of the woods caught Caden's attention. He squinted trying to see who it was.

The man laughed and said something in Spanish.

CHAPTER TEN

He's not a soldier.

Caden's vision cleared enough to see the young man wave a pistol as he sauntered toward him.

He reached for his holster.

It was empty.

His eyes darted, looking for the gun, but couldn't find it in the snow.

The man neared. Tattoos covered his neck and face. His eyes were as cold as the night.

Desperately, Caden tried to come up with a plan.

A smile spread across the man's face. "Beg me for your life," he said with a heavy Hispanic accent.

Caden stared at him without a word.

Bang.

Caden flinched. Blood flowed from the soldier across Caden's legs.

"Beg."

Caden shook his head slowly.

The punk stepped closer and pointed the gun at Caden's face.

An arrow burst from the man's chest. With a lurid scream he staggered backwards, fired the gun into the ground and collapsed in a heap.

Confused, Caden pushed the soldier off his legs and stood. Dizzy, he stumbled as darkness engulfed him.

*　　　*　　　*

Images came in flashes, blood in the snow, soldiers, and a boy with a bow. Gradually Caden became aware of a light shining in his eye. He swatted at it.

"Good, you're awake." Dr. Scott shined the light in Caden's other eye.

"What?" Caden mumbled and again slapped at the instrument.

Hoover stepped into his view. "There was an explosion. We're not sure whether it was an accident or what, but Simon's van would have had both gunpowder and primer in it."

"I remember the blast. The soldier with me?"

"Dead, I'm afraid," Hoover frowned.

Caden nodded and then rubbed his sore head. Realizing he was on a gurney in the hospital hallway he swung his legs over the side and slowly sat up. He struggled to stand, despite the protests of the doctor but, as dizziness caused him to wobble, he quickly sat in a nearby chair. "How long was I out?" He glanced at his arms and legs. "Was I hurt?"

"You just got here," Dr Scott said. "I think you have a grade three concussion. You should be fine, just try to remember that I have better things to do than fix your head every time you decide to hit it against something."

He felt like saying, "Yes ma'am," but just nodded his sore head. "I seem to remember an arrow."

Hoover sighed and shook his head. "I can't decide whether the kid is a hero or a suspect. Zach used a bow to shoot the punk who was threatening you…"

"I'm going with hero," Caden mumbled.

"…but the road the gang was on would have taken them right past his trailer. It leaves me wondering why the kid was in the woods and why was he armed."

"I think you're a little too suspicious, Sheriff." The doctor smiled.

"The kid has a record and I can see him hiding or fencing stolen goods for the gang."

Caden shrugged. "I'm just glad he was there. Did we capture any of the thugs and who exactly are they?"

"We haven't figured that out yet," Hoover said. "The only one we've captured is the one Zach shot."

Setting the chart on the gurney, Scott said, "They're prepping him for surgery now. Dr. Winfield will be operating on him." She shook her head. "This has been one strange year. I'll bet no doctor in town has removed an arrow in over a hundred years."

Looking back to Hoover, Caden asked, "Did you recover any bodies."

"Yes, several."

"One of my soldiers is a police officer from Seattle. He recognized gang tattoos on the shooters at the freeway church last month. I'll have him look at the bodies. I need to talk to Brooks."

"He's still finishing the mop up operation."

Caden looked at Hoover. "Did you bring me here?"

"No, Zach and another soldier brought you in. Brooks said after that he was...well...it seems the soldier with you had a mother here in town."

"I should be there." Caden stood. His head throbbed and he wobbled.

"No. I'm thinking you've had enough action for one night. Brooks can handle the mop-up and you can talk to the mom in the morning. I'll take you home."

He didn't protest.

* * *

Caden's eyes shot open and darted around the room. Quickly, he sat up. Sweat trickled from his brow, his breathing was rapid and shallow. His ears listened for trouble. He was alone in his bedroom. From somewhere in the house came his sister's laughter. A nightmare of battle and death faded from his memory.

Gradually he moved ample covers from his lower body. The chill of the room sent a shudder through him, but the sun shining in the window was bright. For a moment he was angry that no one had awakened him, but his sore head and multiple bruises told him he needed the rest. He stepped to the window. There wasn't a cloud to be seen. The contrast between the blue sky and the snow covered world below was astonishing. Winter in D.C. had always been a nuisance, but here it was striking and beautiful, a portrait in white snow, blue sky and evergreen trees. Remembering the events of last night he was thankful to be there and see it. He sighed recalling the fallen soldier and the visit he would have to make to a mother early this morning.

With the chill in his mood came the sudden realization that it really was cool in his room. He turned on a light just to be sure there was power. He dressed quickly.

Stepping from the room, he nearly collided with Maria. "I was just coming to check on you." In her arms was a well-bundled Adam.

"I'm fine. A little bruised and the head is tender, but I'll live."

"Dr. Scott wants to see you today to make sure there are no clots or other problems." She shifted the baby in her arms.

"I'll put her on the list of people to see. Why is it so cold up here?"

Maria sighed and rolled her eyes. "The news is reporting that prices are going up and your dad is concerned we won't have enough cash to pay the electric bill."

Caden wrinkled his brow.

"He's checking to see if the whole house can be heated with just the wood stove and fireplace."

Apparently the answer is no. Caden rubbed his sore head. "Prices are going up and we need to pay the electric bill with dollars."

"The news calls it inflation, but your dad calls it a monetary collapse."

"Yeah, I've heard others call it that." He squeezed Maria's hand. "After I wash up we can discuss economics and have breakfast beside the fireplace."

She smiled. "Sounds like fun."

Both the chill and the realization that he was hungry hurried his wash and shave. As he finished, Caden remembered a weekend years ago when his father turned off the electricity. It had been a survival experiment, but as a seven or eight year old it was fun, like camping, but with a softer bed. Today's experiment in simple living was just annoying.

Caden swung the door at the bottom of the stairs and the warmth embraced him. *This is why the upstairs is so cold.* He left the door wide open.

In the living room the couch and chairs had been pushed

closer to the fireplace. Sue read in one. Nikki, the puppy, lay lengthwise in front of the fire. A few feet away Adam, on hands and knees, stared at the dog and rocked back and forth.

"Where is everyone?" Caden asked.

Sue set the book on her rounded belly. "Your Mom and Maria are in the kitchen. Dad is in the barn. Lisa is with David at the armory."

Caden smiled as he wandered toward the kitchen. His little sister was moving faster than he was with Maria. *Perhaps, I should change that and finalize plans for the wedding.*

Nikki followed Caden as he headed for the kitchen. Passing Adam, the pup licked the baby across the face.

The kitchen was warm, warmer than the living room, smelled good and Maria was there. He walked to where she stood at the stove preparing breakfast and kissed her on the cheek.

As the two talked, his mother came in with the morning eggs. Nikki laid down under the table.

"Everyone has eaten except you," Maria said, "but I'll have your breakfast ready in a minute. Do you want to eat in here? It's warmer."

Caden nodded.

Trevor entered with a milk pail. "Glad to see you're alive and awake." They talked briefly then the older man headed back to the barn.

His mother poured the milk into several containers and retrieved a strange device from the cabinet. It looked like a cross between a coffee grinder and a blender.

"What's that?" Caden asked.

"A butter churn."

Caden watched his mother whip the milk until Maria brought him a plate of eggs, pancakes, corn bread and coffee on a tray.

Between bites he asked, "Is there any sausage?"

"No," Maria walked back to the counter.

"Bacon?"

"No."

"Bread?"

"Cornbread."

"Maple syrup for the pancakes?"

"No, but we have plenty of butter." His mother whipped the milk in the butter churn.

"Or honey," Maria added.

His stomach grumbled. "Can I get some of each?"

"Sure." Maria brought a plastic container filled with soft white butter and a jar of honey. She pointed to his cup. "We even have cream, but only a little more coffee."

"Really, we're low on coffee? I thought we had plenty."

Maria shook her head. "There's only one can left in the pantry."

The availability of cream and butter rolled around in Caden's mind for a moment. *Of course.* "I guess we're lucky we have the cow."

Maria smiled. "Sue and I named her Bluebell."

Caden smiled back. Naming a cow they might someday eat was a bad idea. "Did you name the calf?"

"Your dad said to wait. I'm not sure why."

Caden grinned, but said nothing. He was nearly done eating when the phone vibrated in his pocket. Looking at the display he saw it was Brooks and quickly answered it.

"I wanted to let you know Sergeant Palmer, the man from the Seattle PD, is on his way to the hospital. He'll check out the tattoos, but he doesn't know enough Spanish to do an interrogation."

"Let the sheriff do that."

"Their only Spanish-speaking deputy was killed during the golden horde chaos…."

"Golden what?"

"Golden horde, that's what people call the mass exodus from the cities during the attacks. The only bi-lingual deputy was killed at the time. They're looking for someone reliable."

Caden looked at Maria. She had spoken only English around him, but he knew her family ancestry was from Mexico. "Maria do you speak Spanish?"

She gave him a confused look. "It's rusty, but yes. Why?"

"We might need your help questioning the guy who tried to kill me."

Her eyes widened and mouth opened, but she said nothing.

"If that is okay with you. Think about it." He looked at the table and spoke into the phone. "Did we have any other casualties?"

"Only the one. The others were just minor wounds."

"The man we lost, his name was Collins, right?"

"Yes, Richard Collins. I visited the mother last night. You don't...."

"She's here in town...a neighbor. I should."

Brooks gave him the address. After breakfast Caden dressed in his class "A" uniform. On his way out he paused in front of a full length mirror making sure every ribbon and insignia were properly placed.

"You look good. Are you going to visit the mother?" Maria stepped into his reflected view.

Caden nodded.

Maria breathed deeply. "I'll interpret if you need me."

"Thank you. Hopefully we won't." He kissed her then walked out the door.

On the way into town, Caden spotted Zach and his sister as he passed the stream where they set their traps. He stopped the car and walked back. "This is the second time I've stopped to thank you."

The boy climbed the bank. Vicki followed with an intrigued look on her face.

Caden shook Zach's hand. "You saved my life last night when you shot that thug with your bow."

"What?" Vicki asked with wide eyes.

Zach ignored her. "I'm sorry the other man died."

"We all are."

"Someone died?" his sister asked.

"It was my fault," Zach said.

"No it wasn't. Why would you say that? You did nothing wrong."

"I could have...should have shot sooner. What was his name?"

"The man who died? Private Richard Collins." He decided not to tell him that he was on his way to console the young man's mother.

As Caden walked back to the car he heard Vicki say, "You shot somebody with your bow? Why didn't you tell me?"

Caden couldn't help but smile. Zach's sister would drag every little detail from him before the morning was over.

As he drove away he tried to remember Zach's age. Hoover said he was a minor...sixteen, that's what he said. Caden bit his lip. If he could find a way to get Zach working at the armory he could keep an eye on him. There were many good male role models there. Maybe together they could provide a bit of guidance. *I'm going to find a way.*

He wondered how recruiting efforts were going. Zach was too young to enlist, but he could hire the boy to help around the unit. Caden stopped and backed the car down the road.

Zach watched the unusual driving with a questioning look on his face.

Caden rolled down the window. "You mentioned once that you've been eating a lot of fish lately. I might be able to diversify your diet. We need some help at the armory, mostly grunt work, cleaning and maintenance. I can pay you in cash or food or a combination.

A surprised looked spread across his sister's face.

"You can start after you're done with fishing each morning," Caden added.

Zach thought for a moment. "Sure, that would be great."

"Good. Report to the front gate tomorrow at 0900." Pressing the gas pedal he drove on toward town.

Caden parked several houses away. His stomach twisted in a knot. He was more reluctant to do this duty than any other, but it was *his* duty, and it was the right thing, the proper thing, to do. If his words could bring any comfort, it was what he had to do and he would never be at peace with himself until he did.

He pulled into the driveway and walked up to the door. *Letters are so much easier than this.*

He knocked.

The door opened.

Eyes that had seen too many tears stared at him.

"Mrs. Collins, my name is Caden Westmore. I was your son's commanding officer and I was with him when he died."

CHAPTER ELEVEN

Zach approached the armory by a path that wound through meadows and a nature preserve. The incline of the trail was more gradual than the road and made a more enjoyable journey.

As he walked through the forest his mind focused on pleasant things, giant fir trees, green moss, ferns and the chirping of birds. The thought of food, other than fish, also lingered in his mind. Pizza, hamburgers and chips would all be nice. But always his mind returned to DeLynn, her blonde hair, cute smile and the fact that she liked him. In all his life he had never met such a nice girl that also liked him.

Growling snapped his mind back to the moment. In the trees up ahead several large dogs tore at the carcass of an animal.

He froze.

Two pit bulls, a German Shepard mutt and at least three others tore at the meat, watched him and snarled at everything.

He suspected the animal being ripped and shredded was a deer, but he wasn't going to try for a closer view.

Slowly, he backed away.

Even when he lost sight of the dogs, he moved with measured deliberation in a wide arc around them and toward the armory. With a sigh, he came out of the woods near the gate and walked up wondering what to say to the man with the big black gun.

"Ah…my name is Zach Brennon and ah…"

The guard checked a list. "The C.O. is expecting you. He's on the far side of the main building or you can go up to his office." The man pointed to a window.

Before he walked away he told the guard about his encounter with the wild dogs. "You should probably warn people."

Entering the compound Zach decided to find Caden, and headed around the main building. He was surprised to see children playing in the grassy field. Rounding the next corner he was startled to see a rifle with the bayonet stabbed into the ground in the middle of the lawn. He took a step, then stopped and stared.

Atop the rifle was a helmet and on either side were boots. A podium and lectern were being set up beside it. From some half-forgotten news report or picture he knew this was a memorial for a fallen soldier. He thought of the man he had seen murdered a couple days before. He stood still, as if at attention, and thought of Richard Collins. *It's probably for him.*

Remembering his sorry performance during the Battle of Olympia and how his hesitation during the gang fight got Collins killed, he felt unworthy to be there. His gaze fell to the ground and he stepped back toward the building.

"I'm glad to see you."

Zach spun around. Caden stood a few feet behind him.

The boy swallowed. "I've seen this before." He pointed to the display. "I know it means someone died, but not much more. Is this for…?" The name caught in his throat.

"Private Collins? Yes it is. It's a battlefield cross. We're having a memorial service for him later today. You should be there."

Zach shook his head. "I was afraid."

"With no training and little experience…anyone would be. I still get scared. I know you said you should have shot sooner, but Private Collins was my man, my responsibility. Only God knows if you could have saved him, but you did shoot and you did save me." Caden's hand rested on his shoulder. "I'm grateful. Don't beat yourself up over what might have been."

Zach had revealed a bit of the sadness that was always with him and felt that Caden's response was sincere. It lifted some of the burden. He nodded. "Where do you want me to help?"

Caden led him to the motor pool.

When it was time for the memorial service, Zach lingered behind the others and found a spot off to the side and hopefully out of view. He didn't want to be seen, and he hoped Caden would not mention him.

The soldiers chatted and smiled with each other as they

gathered on the lawn. More than once he heard the name of the fallen soldier. Their uniforms seemed perfect, their faces calm, confident and resolute as they formed in ranks. He, like an invisible observer, watched what he could never be a part of. *They seem so at home, so much a family.*

"Company, attention!"

Caden stepped to the lectern. "We are here today to honor the memory of a brave young man…"

Zach's eyes fell to the ground. Silently he slipped away.

*　　*　　*

The next morning Caden and Maria strolled into the hospital talking back and forth about nothing in particular. Walking through the maze of pastel colored hallways, they finally found Dr. Scott, Sheriff Hoover and Sergeant Rand, clustered around a monitor at a nurse's station.

They were watching a man handcuffed to a bed. His tattooed face was one Caden would never forget. The man laid quietly, his eyes half open as if bored or sleepy. When he shifted the hospital robe fell to his sides revealing an assortment of tattoos, some elaborate, others simple. A white bandage, high on the right side of his chest, contrasted with his olive skin, and tattoos of blue, black and purple.

"What was his name again?" Caden asked.

With his eyes still on the monitor Sergeant Rand said, "The name on the driver's license is Gonzalo Cruz." His face darkened. "He's covered with Mara Salvatrucha, MS-13, tattoos. They're a notoriously brutal gang."

Hoover groaned.

Caden rubbed his chin. *Great, not just a criminal gang, a vicious one.* Turning to Rand he asked, "What else can you tell me?"

"Not much. They were just getting a foothold in my precinct." He rubbed his chin. "I remember from a briefing that membership estimates ranged up to 70,000 worldwide and 10 to 15,000 in this country."

"A worldwide gang?"

"Most are in central America and the southwest United States."

The sheriff shook his head. "Apparently the northwest is a

new growth area."

"He has a Los Angles address on his driver's license." Dr. Scott sighed. "We may have an even bigger, medical problem."

"What?" Caden asked.

"The influenza outbreak I told you about. They may bring it right to us."

Caden looked back at the monitor. "Why here? Why my town?" He sighed and looked at Maria. "You listen from here. I want him to think he's talking to a bunch of English only Anglos."

Maria smiled. "He will be."

Caden grinned back at her. "Okay, I guess that's true, but you're my trump card." Still smiling he dismissed Sergeant Rand and then turned to Dr. Scott."

"Are we recording?"

She pressed a button below the monitor. "We are now."

Caden turned to the sheriff. "Have you got the ear piece for me?"

Hoover held out his hand. "Wear it like a hearing aid."

While the sheriff handed the microphone and transmitter to Maria, Caden fiddled with the earbud.

"Say something," Hoover said to Maria.

"I feel like a CIA agent."

Hoover nodded and touched his ear. "I heard you." He looked at Caden.

"I heard. Is everyone ready?"

Hoover nodded. "Let's question the punk."

"I'm going, too," Dr. Scott said.

Caden and Hoover looked back at the doctor.

"He may be a murderous thug, but right now he's also my patient."

Caden shrugged and continued down the hall, past the soldier guarding the room. Taking a deep breath he entered the room. "Mr Gonzalo Cruz…."

"Así que estos gringos pendejos ya aprendieron mi nombre."

In his ear Maria said, "Oh, you stupid gringos figured out my name."

"You know English. I've heard you speak it. You're being held under the provisions of martial law. Civilian courts and habeas corpus have been suspended. I am Major Westmore the local military commander. We'd like to ask you a few questions."

With heavy accent he said, "I ain't telling you nothing."

Ignoring his comment, Caden asked, "Your driver's license has a southern California address. When did you arrive here?"

Cruz remained silent

"Why are you here?"

He looked at Hoover. "Para matar policías."

"He says he's here to kill police." Maria advised.

Hoover grunted.

Caden cast him a disapproving glance.

"This would be easier if you spoke English," Hoover said.

With cold calculating eyes Cruz looked at each of the three and grinned.

He's wounded and handcuffed to the bed, but he still wants to convince us he is in charge. Does he really think he's ever getting out of jail? Caden had seen the smug look before. This boldness, or in this case perhaps machismo was the better word, masked a cold evil. *Is it just bravado or is it more? The gang, MS-13, what about them?* Caden turned to Hoover. "We killed the rest of the gang. What can one wounded man do?"

"Somos muchos más y cuando el resto de mis compañeros lleguen de Los Angles, este pueblo, Olympia y Tacoma, todos van a estar controlados por nosotros."

Maria gave a sad sigh in his ear. "He says there are a lot more of them coming up from Los Angles and when they get here they are going to run this region."

Caden put on his best concerned parent act. "I recognized Los Angles and the local towns. Do you have friends or family we should contact in any of those places?"

Cruz sneered, "Todos los del sur de California vienen en camino y cuando lleguen los vamos a poner a ustedes bajo tierra."

"He says that when they get here they are going to run Hansen, Olympia and...."

Locking eyes with Caden he asked, "Where do you live soldier boy?"

Caden could hear Maria's breathing but she had stopped in mid-sentence. He decided to continue. "I'll ask the questions."

"Lo voy a descubrir, te voy a matar, y me voy a quedar con tu mujer y tu casa. Todo lo que sea tuyo pronto será mío. Muy pronto."

No translation came from Maria. Anxious to find out what was happening he stepped toward the door.

"¿Y si tienes mujer, gringo, o te gustan los hombres?"

Caden didn't understand the words, but he heard the venom. He looked back at Cruz with a calm, cold stare.

"Y al que me pego con esa fleche, le voy a pelar el cuero vivo."

Both the doctor and Hoover walked toward the door. Caden looked at Cruz. "Keep him here for now."

"What's the charge?" Cruz shouted.

Caden paused at the door. "See, you do know English." Memories of the previous night flew through his mind, the explosion, hitting the ground, the dying soldier and this thug waving a gun and shooting. "For starters, the murder of Private Richard Collins."

Cruz smirked. "Is that the guy who landed on you?" He made an arching motion with his free hand that ended with, "Splat." He laughed, but then locked eyes with Caden. The thug's face grew dark and angry. "I want a lawyer."

The three walked from the room and returned to Maria at the nursing station.

Only as they approached did Maria lift her gaze from the floor. Tears welled in her eyes.

"What did he say," Caden asked.

Her eyes darted between Caden and Hoover. "Cruz promised to kill both of you and skin Zach alive."

CHAPTER TWELVE

Hoover's eyes widened. "How did Cruz find out that Zach shot him?"

"He hasn't, not yet anyway, but he sure wants to know and then...do what he said."

Caden sighed deeply. "I'm sorry you heard his sociopathic rant, but I'm glad he didn't see you. I have a meeting with the general staff tomorrow in Olympia. While I'm there I'll see about getting help tracking down the rest of the gang."

Minutes later as they exited, Maria stopped and looked up at Caden. "Cruz hates you. He wants to kill you and destroy everything you have...the farm...me."

"He threatened you? How did he know...."

"Not directly. He threatened, 'your woman.'"

He smiled that such an independent person as Maria considered herself his woman. Caden put his arm around her and together they walked toward the car. "Cruz has already committed crimes that warrant death under the martial law edict. I want to hold him now and see what intel we can get from him, but if he tries anything, we'll hold the tribunal and carry out the sentence." He hugged her. "You're safe." But as he looked across the parking lot at the cars, RVs and trailers filled with people more desperate with each passing day, he knew that Hansen was on the knife edge of violence and chaos.

She gave him a long look. "He scares me, but I'm worried about all of us."

He unlocked the car door, and scanned the edges of the lot where a dozen people of varying ages milled about.

Most are probably the families of patients, with nowhere to go now that

Seattle is gone. All looked tired, gaunt and poor, in clothes that had been worn too long without a wash. Looking at a group of men around a fire, he thought of desperation and anger. When several turned and stared at him, Caden said to Maria, "Let's get home."

As they approached the farmhouse Caden squeezed her hand. "So, when are we getting married?"

"I've been thinking about it, but…well, you haven't agreed to a date."

Caden parked and stepped from the car. "Tomorrow."

"What?" Maria said with a chuckle and exited the car. "You said there were meetings and a supply run to Olympia on Friday."

He walked to her side. "The next day then."

She laughed. "Let's give everyone, including me, time to prepare."

"Okay…the first day of spring is in about two weeks. Let's get married then."

The grin faded as her eyes searched his. Then, the hint of a smile returned, but with a bit of sadness that frightened Caden.

"There are times that I want to throw caution and everything my mother taught me aside and just be with you." She leaned up against him, resting her head on his chest. "I've seen so much tragedy, so many people have died in the last six weeks. The night we met we both killed someone."

"They killed your parents. They tried to kill me and Adam."

"I know they deserved to die, but in a saner world we wouldn't be judge, jury and executioner."

"We do what we have to do."

She nodded and looked at him with soft caring eyes. "I guess that's it. I don't want to marry you because I have to. On the day that I know I could walk away from you and not starve, not be killed or raped by some gang or warring armies, that's the day I will marry you."

"There's a new normal. That day may never come."

"It will. As long as there are enough men like you."

She stepped away, but he held her hand. Pulling her back, they kissed.

An hour later, Caden drove toward the armory a bit confused about his engagement. He touched his lips with one finger. *If she's having second thoughts, she has a strange way of showing it.*

Walking toward the main building, he saw Zach and a young private working on a truck engine. He decided to bring Zach along when they went to Olympia. The young man could help load supplies.

Brooks was talking to another soldier as Caden entered the office. With his mind awkwardly drifting between his conversation with Maria and concern about MS-13, he grasped the coffee cup from his desk and returned to the common area. "Why is the coffee pot off?"

A private sitting at a nearby desk said, "Ah, sir…we ran out of coffee yesterday."

With a frown Caden turned back to his office. *One more reason to go to Olympia tomorrow.*

"Here is the requisition list." Brooks followed him. "Some of the medical supplies are for the hospital and some of the fuel is for the sheriff and some of the food is for distribution at the schools, the hospital, the Salvation Army and the Community Church, just west of town."

Caden nodded at the mention of the church his family had attended for years. He took the paperwork and continued on to his desk. He sat down flipping pages of the seemingly endless list of needed items. Finally he said, "Add coffee."

Brooks gave him a doubtful look.

"We won't get half the stuff on this list, but maybe we'll get lucky and they'll have coffee."

Brooks grinned. "I'll add it."

*   *   *

The next morning several trucks and a fueler waited at the armory for the trip to the supply depot. Zach was about to climb into the back of a deuce and a half, when Caden motioned for him to come over. "Keep me company." He pointed. "Ride up here in the SUV.

The boy hesitated, then said, "Sure."

The two sat in the back with a driver and guard in the front. Caden thought getting better acquainted with Zach would be a good use of the hour long trip to Olympia. While he genuinely wanted to know more about the boy, he didn't want to reveal that he had been checking into the young man's background.

Such a "get to know you" talk could start with something like, "So, what does your dad do for a living?" But he knew Zach's father had been murdered and Caden didn't want to open that area of discussion—at least not yet. Finally he settled on, "How has the fishing business been?"

"We won't starve. We're better off than many, but when I have a choice I don't think I'll ever *want* to eat a fish again."

Caden smiled.

The conversation continued with Zach talking about the traps and where to place them in a stream.

"Will you go back to school?"

"Yeah, I want to graduate, but right now we need to eat. I'll go back to school when things get back to normal."

"Will things ever be normal again?"

The soldier in the front passenger seat glanced over his shoulder.

Caden immediately regretted uttering his own doubts.

"I hope so." Zach looked down at the holster on Caden's hip. "Can you teach me how to shoot?"

Caden's wanted to say no, but thought of Cruz and his promise to skin alive the person who shot him with the arrow. *Is it right to tell a sixteen-year-old that someone wants to kill him? The guy is in custody, but what if his friends find out and want to take revenge? Zach has a right to know the danger.* He exhaled slowly. The conversation was not going the way he wanted. "Do you own a gun?"

Zach hesitated. "Sure. My mom owns one, but she isn't very good with it and neither am I. The gang shootout near the house was crazy scary. The world has gone nuts. I need to protect my family."

Caden smiled at the teenage boy. *So young to bear such a burden.* "Would learning to shoot be okay with your mom?"

"Yeah sure, like I said, she owns a gun."

Caden looked into the boy's eyes. *I'm going to ask her anyway.* Then he told Zach about the interrogation of Cruz. "He hates everyone, but he seems to especially loathe me, I guess because I'm the local authority figure and he failed to kill me, and you because you shot him with the arrow."

Zach's eyes had grown slowly bigger as Caden explained.

"Cruz doesn't know your name and I'll never release him, but he and his friends are dangerous." He paused still deciding what to do. He had learned some things about the boy, but not the kind of things he had intended. "If you own a gun you should know how to use it." Caden took a deep breath and let it out slowly. "Okay then, on our range with our weapons and under supervision."

Zach nodded.

"I think I'll have Staff Sergeant Fletcher begin your instruction."

The trip to Olympia went quickly. The highway was clear of abandoned, stripped and burned vehicles and the traffic was light. Caden saw two state patrol cars, some commercial trucks and military traffic, but few private cars.

Gas is hard to find and so expensive, I guess people can't afford to travel.

It had been only a couple of weeks since Caden had been to the city, but the changes were stark. In the convention center parking lot, several dozen Humvees and deuce and a half trucks stood idle. Nearby warehouses served as a supply depot. The convoy pulled in front of the office nearby.

Inside, Caden presented the requisitions.

The supply officer looked over the paperwork and laughed. "Coffee? Are you kidding? You might as well ask for gold." The supply officer chuckled. "Actually, I might be able to get some gold."

Caden shot him a skeptical glance.

"Yeah, from surplus electronics, but there's not an ounce of coffee to be found."

"Well," Caden said with a frown, "fill what you can." He left the depot for the Emergency Operation Center.

*　　　*　　　*

After stepping from the elevator on the third floor of the Wainwright building, Caden was stopped by two guards. They checked his identification against a list and allowed him to proceed to the EOC. The operations center was bigger than he remembered. A large "C" shaped table dominated the center of the room. Lap and desktop computers faced in toward the center with a dozen people in uniform hovering around them. Facing the open end of the table were five large monitors mounted on the wall. Currently they displayed both regional and national news channels. To his right was a long table with a host of communications equipment. On his left was a large oval conference table.

Caden scanned the room for General Harwich, the adjutant general of the Washington National Guard, but didn't see him. It took him a few seconds to spot the duty officer, an army captain. Caden walked over and introduced himself.

"You command the Hansen armory, right?"

"Yes."

Stepping close to a map on the wall the captain pointed to Hansen. "Well, it's good to meet you. General Harwich thinks you've done an excellent job protecting this area. He drew a larger circle from the coast, past Hansen, to the mountains and back to the coast. "Just yesterday he said he wanted to expand your area of control."

"Whoa. Slow down. I came to ask for help, not more headaches."

Caden heard a familiar voice behind him. "We've all got headaches, Major, which one brought you here today?"

He turned and saw General Harwich a few feet behind him. After saluting and shaking hands, Caden briefed the general on the recent gun battle near Hansen and what Cruz had told them about the gang moving up from California.

The general seemed lost in thought for a bit. "The Chinese don't tell us anything that is going on in the areas they control. I doubt they tell the Durant administration anything, but refugees from the southwest are more than willing to talk. The Chinese supply food and medicine and have been very effective in restoring order. Most would call it ruthless. Anyone who loots or robs is shot. If you collaborate and work when, where and how they say, you are given food and shelter. If you don't, they make your life difficult at best, often impossible. There is no room for gang activity in the Chinese zone of control, so gang members leave and join the flow of refugees. We think the Red Army may be…" He seemed to consider his words. "Refugees will be flowing out of the Chinese zone for the foreseeable future."

The general called to a nearby corporal, "Son, get me the current sitrep display of the country. The soldier moved to a computer on the nearby conference table and within seconds a large map of the United States appeared on the display.

As the general walked to it, Caden tried to make sense of what he was seeing. Most of the U.S. east of the Mississippi was colored red. *That's the area under Durant's control.* A red oval also encompassed Denver and Colorado Springs. The Pacific coast from just north of San Francisco to the Canadian border and east to the Missouri and Mississippi rivers were marked in blue. *Those are probably the states that support the new congress.* Iowa, Missouri and Arkansas were split.

Texas, eastern New Mexico and Oklahoma were green. *Texas always did go its own way.* Northern Utah was in purple. *Mormons?* The southwest was maroon. *The growing Chinese zone of control.* Splotches of orange surrounded the cities destroyed by nuclear attack. Most of the orange dots had tails that arced away. *The contaminated zones.* For Seattle that area reached into the Cascade Mountains.

He stared at the display while his gut twisted into a knot. *The nation is falling apart, becoming Balkanized.* Suddenly Caden realized the general was talking.

"…huge wave of refugees heading east out of southern California, Arizona, Nevada and New Mexico into Colorado and Texas, but some are heading north toward us. Most are good people trying to get out of the desert and blast areas. Radiation, water and electrical power are huge issues in the southwest. We expect the population of that region to stabilize at less than half, maybe a third, of what it was before the attacks."

"We can't handle a large influx of refugees. How can those states?"

"They can't. We won't be able to handle the evacuees that make it to the northwest."

"I thought we were getting help from other countries."

"We are. China is abiding by the letter of the treaty and providing aid within their zone of control. Australia and New Zealand have sent food and medicine. Canada is providing significant aid to our region, but the American economy and monetary system is collapsing and dragging the international economy with it. The rest of the world can't prop us up."

"What's going to happen to all those refugees?"

The general drew a deep breath and let it out slowly. "Many

will die."

Caden was startled by the matter-of-fact answer, but tried not to show it.

"But getting back to your issue," the general continued, "the criminals among them won't die easy. Frankly...." He looked around the EOC and then motioned for Caden to join him in the corner.

"We believe the Chinese are using the chaos of the refugees, gangs and jihadists to expand their sphere of influence."

"I thought the jihadists had been captured or killed."

He looked at Caden with tired eyes. "There were more radicals in the Muslim community than we originally believed. I'm meeting with the governor in an hour. Do you want to come along?"

"Most definitely."

CHAPTER THIRTEEN

On the wall of the governor's office hung a large political map of the United States showing hundreds of cities and towns. Red pins marked the cities decimated by nuclear terror.

While General Harwich and Governor Monroe spoke, Caden stared at the map. With each passing moment his mood darkened. As a child he had spent hours gazing at such charts as he planned trips to exciting and faraway places. Now this map and the one in the EOC troubled him. As the other two men talked, he wondered why. Suddenly it occurred to him. Each displayed what had been lost, but in different ways. *This map shows the ideal of what was, a united country, but it isn't anymore. The map in the EOC shows the reality of what is and has been lost.* He sighed.

"Are we boring you, Major?" the general asked.

Caden's face warmed. "No, sorry sir, just thinking."

The governor gestured to the General. "Let me consider what you were saying." Turning to Caden, "Major, I need to speak with you."

Monroe outlined the plan the duty officer in the EOC had mentioned earlier.

"You want me to take over security for most of southwest Washington?" Caden rubbed his jaw.

"Yes, I guess that is basically it."

I came here for help but instead.... Again he sighed. "I need to discuss some recent intel I've learned.

Caden briefed the governor about the murder of Jason Pettit. "He reloaded ammo and sold it in the town market. We think the gang was trying to secure a steady supply of ammunition. We captured one of them alive, but we lost a man during the operation."

71

Caden left his own close call out of it and jumped forward to the interrogation of Cruz in the hospital. "The tattoos strongly suggest he is a member of Mara Salvatrucha, MS-13."

"Why is the particular gang significant?" The general asked.

"They're an especially brutal international criminal gang. They deal in drugs, prostitution, human trafficking, and murder. When we interrogated Cruz he said other gang members were coming and they want to control the area. I believe him and I'm going to need help combating it."

Governor Monroe stared at the map for several moments. Then he slowly turned and met Caden's gaze. "I'm sorry about the loss of your soldier. We've seen the rise of gang activity, and general lawlessness, but mainly in the yellow zone. Your area is relatively peaceful."

"Really?" *Is it, or do I need to complain more?*

The governor rubbed his chin. "We need to restore order to the yellow zone and keep the peace in the southwest region of the state. Our resources are already stretched thin.

"I can't spare police or soldiers for a gang fight that may or may not happen. We have too many emergencies that *are* happening." He paused, but his eyes remained fixed on Caden. "We're planning a major operation to root out gangs and the remaining terrorists. The details are still being worked out, but restoring order just north of your sector should be helpful.

"You should consider yourself lucky. Hansen is pretty well off. It's a garrison town. You have electricity, your infrastructure is intact and you'll soon be growing much of your own food."

"But until then we have a lot of scared and hungry people."

Monroe leaned back in his seat. As he did, he looked tired and older. "Scared and hungry is the new normal." He shook his head. "The FEMA camps are barely under control. Cities like Phoenix, Albuquerque and Las Vegas are dealing with starvation, riots and looting. As the weather gets hotter conditions will get worse"

He paused and shook his head. "There isn't much left to loot in those areas." After another pause he said, "Units supporting the new congress control Wyoming and the Colorado passes. Durant's forces are in a line from Colorado Springs through Denver to Fort

Collins."

Caden wondered why Monroe was telling him this, but said nothing.

"Denver doesn't have electricity, water, or much food. Civilians are streaming out of the city. We expect a major battle there in the next few days."

"I didn't realize that the fighting had spread...that Americans were...."

"Fighting Americans again?" Monroe nodded. "The second Civil War has started."

The governor said the words Caden had struggled to utter.

"Combat isn't widespread and both sides are playing it down. Our supporters...spies...in the east tell us Durant thinks that, with the help of China and Europe, he will win in the long run."

Caden shook his head. "The American economy is collapsing, China, Europe, and the world, are all in trouble. Soon Europe won't be able to help Durant, and China won't spend billions unless they are sure of the outcome. I'm certain resistance is already stronger than China expected."

The governor smiled. "Your quick and accurate analysis is what first caught my attention. The world economy is spiraling into depression and that has weakened Durant's support and limited the aid he receives." The governor cast a wry smile, "However, western Canada, Australia and New Zealand have been very generous to the new congress states.

"Durant has the media locked down in the east, but from what refugees and our spies tell us conditions are worse there than here. The population density is higher and there is less farming. Many neighborhoods of the rust belt and bigger east coast cities are still largely empty, and lawless or under gang control. Good people are moving, if they can." He turned to the map, but his eyes seemed to look far beyond it. "Food aid has slowed as the world economic situation worsens and fighting has hampered distribution. People in the east and the west are going to go hungry. If the situation doesn't change quickly many will starve."

Stepping back to his desk he added, "I don't believe MS-13 would attack a garrison town. It would be foolish, but if they do I'll have backup to you in an hour. That is the best I can do."

*   *   *

Caden let Zach ride back to Hansen with the other soldiers so he could think about all the general and governor had told him. The men had picked up the supplies that were available, coffee was not among them, and he had received a promise of help, but with that promise came responsibility for most of southwest Washington. MS-13, Chinese troops, Durant Loyalists, economic depression, starvation and a new strain of influenza; it seemed almost impossible that the little town of Hansen could survive all the threats.

When the convoy slowed to turn off the freeway, Caden realized they were nearing Hansen. A few miles down the state highway and they would be home. He was tempted to have them drop him off at the farm, but his car was at the armory and he felt he should check on how the day had gone.

Brooks and First Sergeant Fletcher were waiting when Caden walked into the armory office. "How has the day been?" he asked looking at both of them.

"I hope you brought back food. There was a riot at the Salvation Army Church."

Caden's shoulders slumped. "Yes, I've got some, but not enough. Was anyone killed?"

"No," Fletcher said, "but we were called to assist. Two deputies and one soldier were injured by rocks and bottles."

"Six rioters were arrested," Brooks added.

Fletcher sat at the conference table. "The sheriff says assaults and thefts are up. He'd like more help from us."

"I was gone one day. It sounds like things got a lot worse."

Brooks grinned. "On the bright side, the churches are encouraging people to organize community and backyard gardens for when the weather warms and several groups are working on something called a seed exchange.

Caden nodded. "Thanks for ending on a good note."

As Brooks headed out the door Caden said, "First Sergeant, I have something else I need to talk to you about."

Caden explained about Zach.

"So…ah, sir, you want me to babysit a kid?"

Caden sighed. "No, First Sergeant, I don't want you to babysit him. He's been working around here for a few days now, but you have more contact with the men."

"But, you want me to teach him to shoot?"

"Yes, if his mother doesn't object, and from what he says, it sounds like she won't. He saved my life and in the process earned the wrath of MS-13. He needs to know how to defend himself."

"I'm not good with kids."

"He's sixteen. That's just a few years younger than some of the men here."

Fletcher nodded. "But there's a world of difference between a boy in school and a man who volunteers and makes it through boot camp."

"Yes that's true, but I know you have kids."

"Two daughters and they live with their mother in Florida."

"I guess that would make it hard to be a parent."

"My ex said it was as far away as she could get and still be in the country."

Caden grimaced. "Well, you have more experience than me. You don't have to be his dad, just teach him how to safely use a weapon. I'll go by his house and talk with the mother tonight."

Fletcher rubbed his chin. "Yes, sir."

*　　　*　　　*

Caden passed the spot in the road where he nearly died. Using directions Hoover had provided, he continued up the road and within seconds saw the number he was looking for on a mailbox. He turned left onto a narrow dirt driveway and wound uphill till he saw a pastel blue singlewide trailer trimmed in rust. No cars were parked nearby. Dim light came from a single window.

The ancient wooden steps creaked as Caden walked up and knocked. There was no answer, but the door popped ajar with the last knock. "Hello?" Slowly he pulled the door open. "Hello?"

Inside a woman slumped in a living room chair. Concerned she might be ill, or even dead, he stepped in. A lamp cast a pale yellow glow over the room. "Ah, are you all right?" As he moved forward he wondered if he should check her pulse. As he stepped beside her the floor creaked.

Zach's mother snored loudly and belched. The stench of stale booze filled the air.

Caden shook his head in disgust and covered his nose.

She snored again and then opened her glazed eyes for a moment before shifting and returning to unconsciousness.

As Caden turned away he noticed a nearly empty bottle cradled in the woman's arms like a baby. A spilled glass was on the floor beside her. He shook his head. *Hoover said the mom was a drunk, but I hope he's wrong about the boy.* Determined to do what he felt best, Caden left.

*   *   *

The next morning Zach sat in a corner as several men entered the room carrying rifles that looked a lot like the one he stashed in the shed. A couple of the soldiers nodded at him. One even said, "Hi."

Caden had told Zach to come there and that someone would show him how to shoot, but as the men sat around the large table in the middle of the room and began taking apart the rifles, he thought it just looked like work.

He had hoped Caden would show him how to shoot, but it was perhaps too much to expect the commanding officer to do that.

One of the men turned to Zach and asked, "You want to help clean rifles?"

"Ah…someone was supposed to show me how to shoot."

The soldier grinned. "Well, this is how you start. Come on over."

Zach sat beside the soldier who appeared to be only four or five years older.

The man held out his hand, "My name is John Tyler, just like the president."

"Zach Brennon," he said taking his hand.

"This is an M-4 automatic rifle. Go ahead and take it." Tyler picked up another one. "Now do what I do. I'll go slow. Pull the charging handle back like this. Good. Now, press this lever to hold the bolt open. Any rounds in the chamber?

"Bullets? No."

"Check carefully. We don't want to shoot Jason." He pointed to the soldier at the end of the table.

"Yeah," Jason said, "check really good."

A man old enough to be Zach's father entered the room. He had seen him around the armory, but the man had ignored him.

"Hey, First Sergeant are you going to help us clean rifles?" John asked.

The man sat across from Zach. "Yeah, I think I will." He picked up one and pulled back on the charging handle.

John turned to Zach. "Okay if the chamber is empty release the bolt. Make sure your fingers are clear and press here."

The bolt slammed forward startling Zach. *Nope, don't want my fingers in the way.*

Fletcher looked across the table with a serious expression. "So, you're the kid that shot the gangbanger with the bow."

Zach felt his face flush as every eye turned to him. "Yeah, I guess so."

The older man nodded. "Pretty good shooting. Maybe you could teach these knuckleheads how to shoot a bow."

"My aim was off," Zach said with a shake of the head. "I was nervous and should have shot sooner. Maybe if I had, the other guy, Collins, might have lived."

No one spoke for a moment.

Fletcher broke the silence. In a low soft voice he said, "Private Collins was a member of this Squad. I'm sure everyone here wishes they had been able to help, but no one knows the future. No one expected that crazy thug to wait in the woods. No one expected you to be there. You could have stayed in your house or ran the other way. All the other civilians that night did, but not you. Even though no one called, you came, and because you did Major Westmore, a good officer...a good man, lived. Don't second guess yourself. You did well."

Several soldiers nodded their agreement.

Tears welled in Zach's eyes. *Not here. Not now.* He looked down and focused on cleaning the rifle. By the time they finished the job, Zach was field stripping and cleaning weapons without asking how from those around him.

"Tomorrow these guys are going out on the rifle range." Fletcher said looking at Zach. "Do you want to go shooting with them?"

"Yes sir."

"Don't call me sir, I'm enlisted."

Zach was confused, but recalled how several of the men had

referred to him. "Yes, First Sergeant."

Fletcher stood and smiled. "You might be okay, kid."

CHAPTER FOURTEEN

The rifle Zach had kept after the Battle at Hansen lay field stripped on a blanket in front of him. Behind the shed next to his home, he felt safe from the prying eyes of his mother. These last couple months she rarely went out, and never came this direction.

Because of his training at the armory, he knew the rifle was a semi-automatic AR-15. Yesterday, when he said he had such a weapon, First Sergeant Fletcher gave him a cleaning kit. So, this morning he awoke extra early to set the fish traps. That provided the time to field strip and clean the rifle. Looking at the black rags, he knew the gun had *really* needed it.

He also discovered that there were twenty-eight rounds in the magazine. Over the next few minutes he reassembled and dry fired it once to ensure he had done everything properly.

Pleased with the condition of the weapon he considered his, he stood.

The crunch of gravel under foot came from the driveway.

It's probably Vicki. Holding the rifle in one hand, he slipped the magazine in his pocket and moved cautiously around the shed. If his mother had ventured outside, he didn't want to be seen.

The sound of footfalls on the stony ground told him the person was close. He peeked around the corner of the shed into DeLynn's face.

She stifled a scream. "What are you doing with that gun?"

"Cleaning it. Sorry I startled you."

"You could have killed me."

He grinned and pulled the magazine from his pocket. "I didn't point it at you and the rounds are in here."

She cast a confused look at the magazine and then at him. "I didn't know you owned a gun. Did you get it from the Armory?"

"No, they don't give them away, it's mine." He opened the shed door. From inside he said, "But, I do have something for you from the armory. He stashed the rifle in its hiding place and then slung his bow over his shoulder. As he exited he grabbed his quiver and a bag with several MRE's in it. He held out the bag. "Here."

"I don't want you to get in trouble for taking things."

He laughed. "This they give to me. Part of my pay is in rations."

She sighed and took the bag with a sad smile. "My parents dislike you, but you've been good to them and me." She leaned forward and kissed him.

"Don't sugar coat it. Your dad hates me."

DeLynn looked at the ground. "No one in Dad's law firm has worked since the attacks. There isn't much need for contract and business law. We wouldn't eat if it wasn't for you."

"I kind of understood it before. I know I have a bad rep. But now after the terrorist attacks and chaos, I really get it. He's trying to protect you. I've been trying to protect my sister, you and Mom." He shook his head. "Helping you is easy. Helping my mother is the hardest."

"I think your mom is hurting."

"About what?"

She shrugged. "Your dad getting killed?"

"That was a long time ago and why would that make her drink?"

"Sometimes that's how people show their hurt…"

Zach shook his head. "A stupid way to do it."

"…or maybe it's that Bo guy you've told me about. He's got to be a bad influence."

Zach nodded. "He's just bad." He hugged and kissed her. "I've got to go. I'm on the rifle range today."

"Really? Why the bow then?"

"The guys want to see me shoot it." As he turned to head into the woods his sister stepped out onto the porch of their trailer. "What's up, Sis."

"I thought I'd talk to DeLynn."

He looked hard at his sister.

"Don't worry. I won't tell her you get teary eyed during romantic movies."

He gritted his teeth.

"Just kidding. Go on, I promise to be good. Unless you want to stay for some girl talk."

When it came to DeLynn, his first girlfriend, he wasn't sure he could trust his sister. *Mom is sleeping off a bender so at least DeLynn won't see her.* He was apprehensive, but there was little he could do. With a sigh and a wave to both, he trotted into the forest toward the armory.

* * *

Zach turned the compass left and right. "What's this called again, First Sergeant?"

Fletcher sat on a nearby rock outcropping at the edge of a meadow. "Orienteering." An amused grin grew on him.

He looked at the map and then at the compass. "I don't need these things to find my way around here."

"So, you think you could walk out without getting lost?" Fletcher asked.

Zach nodded and pointed. "That way is north."

"That's easy. You can use the sun to figure that out. Which way is the armory?"

"Over there about six miles." Zach pointed.

Fletcher smiled. "More like seven. Which way to the rally point?"

Zach turned to the side. "Go over the next hill and down to the creek then follow it to where it joins the river. Follow the river upstream to the rally point at the bridge."

"A roundabout way to get there but, okay, you know where you are." For several moments the first sergeant gazed at his surroundings with a contented smile. "Come sit with me for a while."

Zach sat on the rock and admired the view with him, while wondering why he wasn't in more of a hurry to meet up with the other soldiers.

"Beautiful land isn't it."

Zach nodded.

"This parcel connects with the national forest on the south and west. The river goes along the east side."

"Yeah, great hunting in this area."

"You've hunted on my land?

"Your land?" Zach felt his face flush. "I didn't know...I'm...."

Fletcher laughed. "I don't care. Enjoy yourself."

When Zach's face felt normal again, he said, "This is a nice place."

Fletcher pointed. "You can't see the spot from here, but the meadow goes down to a road. A little creek runs out of the hill to nearby culvert."

Zach nodded he knew the spot.

"I was going to build a house there before...well, before my marriage ended."

Embarrassed at the openness of the first sergeant, Zach sat silent for a few minutes. Finally he said, "Shouldn't we head to the rally point?"

Fletcher shook his head. "No hurry. I told the sergeants to let the new guys get lost for a while."

*   *   *

Caden and Brooks sat in the office reviewing plans and rosters.

Suddenly, the sound of gunfire roared.

Brooks stood, stretched, and walked over to the window. "We don't have a surplus of ammo. Should we be wasting...?"

"It's not wasted." Caden interrupted. "I told Fletcher to limit range time, but the soldiers, especially the new ones, need to practice so they're familiar with their weapons."

Turning from the window, Brooks nodded. "Did you hear that Durant froze wages and prices today?"

"Yeah, I heard." Caden leaned back in his chair. "President Nixon attempted a wage and price freeze. It didn't work then and won't work now."

Brooks looked doubtful.

"Since the Roman Emperor Diocletian, rulers have tried it during economic emergencies, but all it does is increase barter and force people into the black market. Some of the states are already moving to nullify Durant's order."

"Can they do that?"

Another volley of gunfire thundered.

"Thomas Jefferson thought so, the courts said no, but with the country splitting apart...." He shrugged and then was silent for a moment. "Durant also indexed mortgages to the inflation rate."

"What does that do?" Brooks asked.

"As inflation goes up so does your mortgage."

"Then it won't affect me," Brooks said, "Unless I decide to buy the armory room I live in. Will it hurt your family?"

"No. When Dad inherited the farm it had a mortgage, but he worked hard to pay it off years ago."

"Your father was wise."

"I never thought so when I was growing up. I believed my whole family was a bunch of rural hicks, with some nutty ideas about survivalism, but having the farm and all that is there has been a blessing."

More shots resounded.

Brooks stared out the window for a moment. "Mortgage indexing might save the banks, but people will be angry when they see what they owe going up and up. I think it will cause more riots."

"Middle-class homeowners aren't the rioting type."

"They already have down at the Salvation Army Church."

Caden nodded. "Good point. Hunger causes riots. We're all going to lose weight before the harvest. Freezing prices and indexing mortgages will just anger people even more."

A myriad of problems and frustrations kept Caden from focusing on the folders and clipboards before him. He tossed the pen on the desk. "Enough paperwork! I'm going to see how the men are doing."

Caden watched from behind as seven men and one boy fired down range. Zach hit the torso of the man shaped target more often than Caden expected. On the table beside Caden was a bow and quiver. He motioned for the First Sergeant to come to him. "What's this for?"

"Zach is going to demonstrate it for the men. I figure it's a good skill for them."

"How is Zach doing?"

He grinned slightly. "The boy is green, but teachable."

*   *   *

Zach dropped a couple of MREs into his backpack.

"They actually pay you with those?"

He nodded. "Part of the pay is money, part is food."

"If you call that food."

"It's not so bad. A lot of people would be glad to have them."

The soldier shook his head and walked away.

Zach hoisted his pack onto his back, thankful the day was ending. He had spent much of the morning in the woods and shooting on the range. That had been fun, but afterwards the day was mostly cleaning things, rifles, floors and miles of brass and stainless steel.

But his work had started well before dawn, with a cold breakfast in a frigid trailer. He had let Vicki sleep in. Even before the first rays of the sun peeked over the valley he was setting fish traps along two streams. Then, loaded with equipment and fish, it was back to the trailer to change clothes. He smiled as he recalled the meeting with DeLynn in the driveway. *I hope Vicki didn't talk much about me.* He made a mental note to pry information about that from his little sister.

With his bow slung across his back, he ran through the forest. The trail was dark, but he knew the way to Hansen and Library Park where his sister would be packing up after a day of selling fish.

Coming out of the woods, he stopped and took a deep breath. His body ached and cried for rest. *Just a little more now. The day is nearly over.* Once again at a trot he headed down the sidewalk.

Zach moved against the flow of people at the park. Most were done with the work of surviving the day and now headed home. For him the last chore, helping his sister close down the stall, was still ahead.

He knew the location well and scanned ahead for a glimpse of his sister as he neared. Zach spotted Bo first of all and groaned inwardly. He didn't want to deal with him tonight. Then the potbellied lowlife turned.

Zach saw that he was holding Vicki by the arm

Bo's voice was low like a growl, but Zach couldn't make out the words.

Fear etched Vicki's face.

Bo raised his free hand.

Vicki cringed.

In a well-choreographed flurry of motion Zach grabbed his bow, nocked, drew and aimed an arrow. "Let go of her Bo!"

A semicircle of wide eyed people formed around the three and was only open on the receiving end of Zach's arrow.

Fixing his eyes on Zach, Bo raised both arms as if surrendering.

Vicki ran toward her brother.

"Your family owes me for the beverages and other stuff I've been providing that mother of yours."

"We owe you nothing. Keep your hands off my sister and leave."

"Leave I shall boy, but you owe me the money." Bo turned and walked into the darkness.

CHAPTER FIFTEEN

As he and Vicki packed up their buckets, knives and other items from the booth, Zach felt as if a thousand eyes watched. But whenever he looked, they quickly turned away.

On one shoulder Zach carried his bow and quiver. On the other he heaved the last load of supplies from the fishmonger stall. Together with his sister, he walked from the market. "What exactly did Bo want?"

"He said it was time to pay for the stuff he gave Mom. I said we didn't have any cash, gold or silver…"

"We don't…well, not much anyway."

"Yeah, I said we're just getting by. But that isn't what he is after. He wants you to get stuff from the armory."

Zach paused in surprise and then shook his head.

"That was when you showed up. I'm really glad you did."

As they walked along the street, Vicki turned toward a wooded lot. Zach stopped her. "Let's stay in town under the streetlights as long as we can. I'd rather meet Bo here than in or at the edge of the forest."

As they reached the outskirts of town the lights became few and the one up ahead was out. A skinny dog ran into the shadows. The world was silent except for the sound of a single car.

Zach looked over his shoulder and even in the dim light recognized the gold Cadillac sedan that Bo had won in a poker game. He dropped the duffle bag and readied the bow.

"Let's run," Vicki said.

The car pulled past and parked along the curb.

"To late for that, Sis."

A burly man stepped out from the driver's side and then Bo

exited from the back. "Hey boy, did your sister tell you about my business offer?"

"That I steal stuff for you? Yeah, she did."

"It's more than that. I want…."

"Don't touch my sister," Zach growled.

Bo smiled. "Sorry about that. My business partners are eager to move this endeavor forward." He took a deep breath. "This could be a profitable venture for both of us. I need someone inside the armory to provide information, gun parts, ammo, brass, magazines and the like. You will be paid well."

"You do know they lock those things in a vault, don't you?"

"You're a bright boy, you could figure something out. Just imagine, no more fishing. You can buy your food and whatever else you want."

He sighed. *No more fishing. No more eating fish.*

"Zach?" his sister said softly.

He turned and smiled at her. She seemed to be able to read his mind at times like this and pull him back from the worst that he could be. "Don't worry, sis." Looking at Bo he shook his head. "No."

"Your mom has been getting more than booze from me these last few weeks. In a day or so she'll beg you to cooperate with me.

Like a volcano, rage rose through him and boiled over. He snapped the bow to the ready.

The burly man pulled a gun.

Vicki screamed, "No!"

"Let's all just calm down," Bo spread his arms. "Think about my offer. I'll be by in a day…or so."

As the two men stepped back to the car, Zach said, "I'll never do business with you."

"I'm asking now. Next time I won't."

As the car pulled away Zach said to Vicki, "Come on, let's hurry. I have a lot of questions for Mom."

When the two got home their mother was sitting on the floor rocking back and forth and staring at the fire in the woodstove."

"Mom, we need to talk," Zach said.

She shook her head and rocked even faster.

Scattered on the floor were several pill bottles and small plastic bags. All empty.

Zach stared at the mess on the floor. "Mom, what did you do?"

Tears welled in Vicki's eyes and she sniffled.

Speaking in a whisper his mother looked at Zach. "Bo told me what he wanted from you. He used me to get at you. This is better."

Zach dropped to his knees beside her. "No, it's not."

"Yes it is." She said with determination. "On that night, that awful night, we had an offer…someone wanted to buy the store…but your dad didn't want to sell." Tears flowed down her cheeks. "I should have been there…I should have been working that shift, but we argued. I said I wasn't going to work there anymore. I should be dead…me…not him." She looked at Zach with glazed eyes. "I'm sorry I've been such a bad mother. If I could trade places with your dad I would." She smiled at them and seemed to let go of a deep sadness. "It is better this way."

For the first time in years Zach hugged her. "No Mom, don't say that."

"I've wanted to do this for so long." Her eyes lost focus. "I finally did it." She collapsed on the floor unconscious.

Moments later Zach banged on DeLynn's door.

It opened a mere two inches with the chain still latched. "What do you want?" DeLynn's father said irritably.

Zach gasped for breath. "Please…I need to phone…It's my mother…."

"No. Get off my property."

"She's unconscious…I think she's dying. We don't have a phone."

The older man stared at him with a face of stone. "She probably just passed out! You and your friends stay away from my daughter."

From inside Zach heard DeLynn's voice. "Daddy, can't you see, this is serious?"

He wanted to pummel the man and steal the car, but instead Zach turned and ran downhill across the snow covered lawn toward the next house several hundred yards away.

A mechanical sound caught Zach's attention as he ran. The garage door of DeLynn's home creaked up. The Hollister's red sedan rocketed out, just clearing the bottom of the rising door.

"Come on!" DeLynn shouted. "Jump in."

He did and together they headed back toward the blue trailer and his unconscious mother.

*　　　*　　　*

Caden drove leisurely through Hansen on his way home. In many ways the street looked normal. Lights were on in homes and businesses. Televisions flickered in some windows. Despite the darkness and cool weather, children played and rode bikes.

However, there were no other cars on the road and many more adults on bikes than he recalled from earlier times. Trash collection was less often now because of gas shortages, so garbage overflowed the bins at many homes. The smell of wood smoke floated in the air.

In the cup holder beside him, his phone rang. He picked it up and saw it was the sheriff. "What's up?"

"There's been a break-in at the school. My deputies are out east of town. Brooks said he would send some men, and that you might be near the school."

"I'm coming up to it now. I'm just over a block away on Main Street."

"You didn't pull over to take my call?"

"Ah…."

The sheriff laughed. "Wait for me. I'll be there in two minutes."

The sound of a car engine brought attention that Caden didn't want, so he parked. He set his phone to vibrate and then stepped from the vehicle. Near the school a dog barked. In the distance came the laughter of children. Otherwise the night was still.

He stood in the shadows a few feet from his car. Another dog barked nearby and then others until a frantic chorus filled the night.

Caden was certain the dogs had detected the break-in. He pulled his gun from the holster and, staying in the shadows, walked gradually forward.

Within seconds he heard a car engine and turned to see the

sheriff drive up and park with neither lights nor siren on.

Caden stepped from the shadows.

With a wave of his arm, Hoover motioned for Caden to follow.

Together they ran down the street, turned and crept up an alley.

The sheriff stopped and pointed to the greenhouse behind the school. Caden recalled from his days of attendance that the Future Farmers of America club and various science classes used the large commercial grade structure.

Caden couldn't see much in the darkness, but then, inside the greenhouse, he saw a beam of light and then another blink on then off.

Flashlights? Turned on and then off? Are people so hungry that they are stealing from the school greenhouse?

Caden looked for anyone on guard, but saw no one.

Hoover whispered, "Take cover there." He pointed to an old and very wide tree. Then, with his gun at the ready, he moved to a nearby stone fence.

From behind his tree, Caden stared at the door wondering how many were inside. Hoover might have been wondering that also. He seemed content to wait for the soldiers to arrive.

The rattle of boxes and stumbling steps indicated there were at least two people inside.

A flashlight flicked on and off.

"Stop that," an angry male voice commanded. "We'll get caught."

"I can't see!"

"We've got everything worth taking," Another said. "Let's go."

The doors opened.

"This is the sheriff! Stop! Put your hands up!"

A shot rang out.

Then another.

Thud.

A scream thundered from the darkness.

"Turn on your flashlights," the sheriff commanded.

"You'll shoot us!"

"If you don't turn them on, I might."

When their lights were on Caden saw the group huddled together.

Hoover turned on his light, pointed it at them, and called for an ambulance.

"Back inside the greenhouse." Hoover commanded as he approached.

Caden took one of their flashlights, examined the fallen man and applied pressure to his wound. "He'll need that ambulance, but he might live."

Sirens wailed in the distance.

Looking over those standing, Caden saw one woman and three men. They were all clearly scared, but not hardened criminals.

"The government needs to do something. We're starving," one said.

"We've got families to feed," the woman added.

"You guys are hoarding all the food."

"We have rights!"

"Yeah, our children have a right to eat!"

"Everyone has a right to eat."

There was real hunger in the community, but these men appeared able and, while they might have been hungry, none was starving. They could all do something more useful than waiting for assistance or resorting to theft.

"You don't have a right to steal, but we will feed you—in jail," the sheriff said. "You're all under arrest." He pulled a handful of zip ties from his pocket.

*   *   *

In the backseat of the Hollister family car, Vicki cradled the head of her mother.

Zach looked over his shoulder from the passenger seat. "Is she still breathing?"

Vicki nodded as tears rolled down her cheeks.

Zach sighed. "We'll be at the hospital soon." He turned his gaze to DeLynn. She had a white knuckle grip on the steering wheel. "Do you know the way?"

She nodded. "I drove to town with Dad several times, but

never on my own."

"You're not alone now." Zach looked ahead, conflicted. He wanted her to go faster, but was scared that she might and slide off the icy, unsanded road. Taking his eyes away from the winding country lane for just a moment, he looked at her again. The muscles of her neck were tense as she stared straight ahead. Still, she was beautiful. "Thanks for doing this."

"My dad is a jerk."

"He doesn't know I'm the one giving you the fish and the rations does he?"

She shook her head. "He's so proud. I was afraid he would rather starve and Mom and I with him, but I will…I will tell him."

For some reason the fact that she hadn't told him hurt Zach, but all he said was, "It's okay."

Moments later he sighed as they turned from the narrow road that led away from their homes and onto the wider and straighter avenue into town. It was the same street he and his sister had encountered Bo on less than an hour before. Glancing back at his mother, rage boiled within him. *I'm going to kill you, Bo.*

CHAPTER SIXTEEN

Zach rubbed his eyes as DeLynn stepped into the waiting room. "Hi."

"Any word from the doctors?"

He yawned and shook his head "She's still unconscious and in intensive care. What time is...?" He looked at his watch. "I'm late. The fish traps need to be set. Why didn't anyone...."

"Relax. Vicki and I did it this morning."

He blinked. "You in waders, standing in the middle of a freezing stream placing a fish trap?" He smiled. "That must have been a sight."

In a mock indignant tone she said, "Vicki says I did just finc—believe it or not." She sat in the chair next to him. "I spent the night at your place. I'm still pretty mad at my dad. I don't want to go back home." She looked him in the eye. "Can I move in with you?"

Zach stared at her while fireworks lit the black sky of his life. He wanted to shout, 'yes,' but reality's rain dampened his jubilation. *Her parents will hate me more than ever. They'd never stand for it. Her moving in with me would confirm all they already think of me.* "Ah...well...if you did your dad would never approve of me."

"I don't care."

"You will someday, and I would like his approval. I don't want him thinking I'm a bad influence and I've corrupted you."

She giggled at that. "I've never met such a good bad guy."

"I've made some bad choices, but I want to make the right ones with you. If you need time away from your dad, stay with Vicki as long as you want, but I'll bunk at the armory."

DeLynn frowned, but nodded.

"I better get going. It's a long walk to the armory."

"I'll take you. I still have Dad's car."

"You better get it back to him before he has you arrested."

"I will—tomorrow."

As they stepped from the room, Zach looked her up and down. "You might look good in orange."

She thumped his arm with her fist. "I'm not sure I'd want you to join up, but you'd look nice in uniform."

"Don't worry. They won't let me for a couple of years." He looked around. "I want someone here in case the doctors have news. Where's Vicki?"

"She's coming. I told her to give me a minute to talk to you."

Zach sighed deeply and took her hand as they walked down the hall and out of the hospital.

As DeLynn drove toward the armory, Zach considered what to do about Bo. He tried to be rational, but he kept drifting back toward plans that involved torture, murder or both.

Several squads were finishing their morning run as DeLynn pulled up to the post gate.

One soldier smiled and said, "I wish I had more friends that looked like her." He gestured at those with him. "And less that looked like you guys."

Many nodded.

"Too good for you. What's her name?" another asked with a grin.

"What's her phone number?"

Zach's face warmed and he was glad she was already headed away.

"Why would she be interested in any of you smelly knuckleheads?" the First Sergeant asked. "Get showers and then clean the barracks. The XO will inspect at 0900. Zach, come with me."

As they walked away Fletcher said, "Don't let those guys bother you. I'm sure she's a nice girl."

"She is, First Sergeant. The best."

"Then treat her good. That's one thing I've learned." He handed the boy a sheet of paper. "Here are your duties for today. If you get done, second squad is practicing with pistols this afternoon."

Zach looked up at Fletcher and nodded. As he gazed at the

older man in his combat uniform, Zach recalled DeLynn's comment that he would look good in one. "First Sergeant, could I get a uniform?"

"You're not in the military, so why do you want one?"

He didn't want to say it was to impress his girlfriend. "Ah…cleaning. Most of my clothes are either too nice or worn out. ACUs would be good for working, polishing brass, cleaning weapons and other stuff around here."

Fletcher shrugged. "One thing we have a surplus of is uniforms. I'll get you some, but no rank or insignia—and keep'em clean."

The boy nodded and headed off to his first job with a smile.

*　　　*　　　*

Caden sat at his desk reading papers while a radio played softly in the background.

Maybe paperwork isn't so bad. When I have time for it, the day has gone well. He signed the report and moved it from the pile in front of him to the growing stack on his left.

All morning the station had played a mixture of news, commentary and music. He had heard all the news, so the radio was merely blocking the noise of the world around him.

Another paper moved to the left.

Ominous tones ushered from the radio. Followed by, "Breaking news!"

Caden turned to listen.

"Senators and representatives of the re-established congress met for the first time today in Cheyenne, Wyoming. In addition to passing a number of resolutions opposing recent executive orders, the Senate has refused to ratify the Treaty of Mutual Friendship, Aid and Cooperation with China. In a joint resolution the new congress asked countries of the world to continue providing aid, but not seek economic or political control of American resources or sovereign territory. There has been no comment yet from the Durant administration in New York."

Caden ignored the litany of reporter remarks as he mulled the news. Turning from the radio, he noticed Brooks standing in the doorway.

"What do you think about that?" the XO asked.

"Treaties must be ratified by the Senate." Caden leaned back in his chair. "I think the new congress outmaneuvered Durant."

"Then maybe there won't be a civil war."

Caden shrugged. "If Durant recognizes the authority of the new congress there won't be, but do you see that happening?"

The XO's shoulders slumped. "No."

*　　　*　　　*

The sun was low in the sky casting long dark shadows across the ground when Zach, clad head to foot in a montage of camo uniform parts and hunting clothes, crawled on his belly from the woods onto a rock outcrop across from Bo's home. He had never been in the house, never wanted to, but from there he could observe it. First he would learn the routine of the man who had put his mother in a coma and then he would extract judgment.

The living room was dimly lit and the house appeared unoccupied as Zach peered through the scope. Bo mentioned that he had inherited the large two story home on a secluded road at the edge of town. The backyard sloped down to a lake. Other homes were nearby, but far enough away for privacy. Bo's inheritance would make any family in town a nice home, but Bo boasted it was merely a place to sleep and make deals. He seemed always to be making deals. Zach knew the crook was into drugs, booze and guns. What else, he didn't know.

Zach was certain the house was also a place to show off. Bo was a small-town hood, but he played the part well. He had never been arrested; he owned a nice house, a fancy car and had enough money to do what he pleased. Zach hated him and envied all he owned.

A black Chevy drove up and parked in a shadowed area near the home, but no one got out. *That's weird.* The car had a clear view of Bo's house. *Is someone else keeping an eye on Bo?* Zach looked through the scope at the car, but darkness hid whoever was inside.

He quickly lost interest in the car and returned his attention to the house. Minutes slipped away with nothing happening. *This isn't accomplishing anything.* Still he stayed. He wanted to see the man he hated and begin the stalking of his prey.

It seems more exciting on TV. He sighed and waited.

The sound of a car caught Zach's attention. Within seconds

Bo's gold Cadillac sedan came down the road and pulled in the driveway.

The Chevy roared to life and streaked into a blocking position behind the Cadillac. Four men jumped out waving pistols and surrounded Bo and his bodyguard.

It was hard to see detail in the fading light, but Zach, looking through the scope, was sure the men were Hispanic with multiple tattoos on their necks and much of their faces.

Bo tried to say something, but one of the guys pushed him and shouted, "We don't have time for this!"

One guy seemed to be in charge, shouting and pushing. Bo responded, but Zach couldn't make out the words.

An involuntary shudder went through Zach as he remembered the night he shot Cruz. *Are these guys MS-13?*

"We paid you, but so far we got nothing but promises. You better deliver or, I swear man, I'll cut your throat." In a flash a knife was at Bo's neck.

Bo stumbled backwards mumbling.

Zach pressed his eye into the scope.

The gang members walked back toward their car.

What is going on? Zach crawled back into the woods. *Maybe I won't have to kill you, Bo.*

CHAPTER SEVENTEEN

Zach stood over his mother. The steady beep of the cardiac monitor and her slow regular breathing assured him she was still alive. Delynn and Vicki slept, leaning awkwardly against each other in the corner. Usually he liked this time of the evening when darkness signaled the end of the day and there was time to think. However, these last four days, as he watched his mom hover between life and death, the darkness of dusk blackened his mood and thoughts.

The door squeaked and he looked over his shoulder. A woman doctor entered, she always seemed to be somewhere nearby. He wondered if she ever left.

After a moment of small talk, she smiled weakly. "We need to make some decisions this weekend. Is there anyone else, an adult, I should talk to?"

"No, my dad is dead. My sister and I are all the family she has."

The doctor sighed. "I see…well…it's been four days and…."

Anger flared in Zach. "She's not going to wake up, is she?"

"She's stable, breathing on her own. I'm hopeful she will improve…."

"What are you saying?"

She sighed. "There is nothing more we can do for her and…ah…well, the hospital is overcrowded. We need the bed."

Zach looked at his mother for several moments. Anger eased as worry replaced it. "Is there a place she can be taken care of?"

"Normally, yes, but since the attacks those facilities…well…the people who work there have their own families. The hospital is also very short staffed." The doctor's whole body seemed to sag. She sat down with a sigh. "If your mother remains stable, she will need to go home."

"I see," Zach said. "I'll need time to make plans and arrangements."

"Of course. We'll talk again on Monday."

The young man looked at the girls still sleeping in the corner and then, as he thought about the current problem, a dark plan of vengeance formed in his mind. He would come back later and discuss arrangements for his mother with Vicki but, with one last look at Delynn, he turned to leave.

The slow boil of rage pushed out reason. *MS-13 or me—one of us is taking you down, Bo.*

*   *   *

His father flipped between news channels as Caden walked into the living room on a chilly Saturday morning. The smell of eggs and cornbread filled the room.

Looking over his shoulder, Dad gave him a nod.

Generally Caden was interested in the news, but this morning breakfast had the stronger call. Still he said in passing, "What's going on in the world?"

"Durant just finished speaking."

"I don't care what he has to say."

His father nodded, "In other news, North Korea claims the south is preparing for war. India and Pakistan are threatening to nuke each other and China says it's going to annex Taiwan and a bunch of islands in the South China Sea."

Maybe I didn't need to know about all that either. Following the aroma into the kitchen, Caden greeted his mother and sister. Nikki lay under the dinner table apparently enjoying the warmth of the room and the scraps that might be forthcoming. When Caden stayed and sampled the cornbread, his mother ordered him out.

"How come Nikki gets to stay and I don't"

"The *dog* doesn't get in the way."

"Maybe if I crawled under the table with her," he mumbled heading for the door. Then he stopped. "Where's Maria?"

"Collecting eggs."

Caden nodded. "I have come to appreciate the lowly chicken."

While stirring scrambled eggs, Lisa said, "More and more

we're eating what we have here on this place."

"Maybe we should raise more animals," their mother said.

Glancing at the pantry door, Caden asked, "Do we have enough food on the farm for all of us until harvest time?"

His mom opened the door and flipped on the light. The room was the size of a large walk-in closet with well stocked shelves of home and commercial canned goods, bags of flour, rice, noodles, and boxes of cereal and sacks of potatoes.

"Is that enough?" Caden said.

She shrugged. "It was supposed to be a year's supply for Trevor and me and with eggs from the chickens and vegetables from the garden, maybe enough for Lisa too, but now...."

Now there is me and Maria, and Adam and Sue and soon her baby.
Caden walked slowly into the living room and paused by his father. "Other than Durant's speech, what's happening in this country?"

Still looking at the TV he said, "Marine and Army units loyal to the New Congress have nearly surrounded Denver. Durant's forces are retreating to Colorado Springs. Otherwise, most of the news is about the economy and the inflation problem. The local media says that the price of essential goods and services has quadrupled since the terrorist attacks. The east coast media talks about hoarding and price gouging, but I think everyone just figured out that the money really wasn't worth much."

"We still need cash for some things," Caden said.

Trevor nodded. "Yes, taxes and bills, but fortunately not as much as most people. We have a well, so no water bill. We have a septic system, so no sewer bill and we can heat the house with the wood stove and fireplace so our electric bill is lower."

"My room has been pretty chilly these last few days."

Before Trevor could answer the front door squeaked open.

Maria entered. In tight faded jeans, a plaid shirt and holding a basket of eggs she looked like a pin-up for The Grange.

As she neared him they kissed and he wrapped her in his arms.

"Mind the eggs," Maria said.

Caden relaxed his hug.

"Maria, was that you?" His mother called from the kitchen. "How many eggs did you get?"

"Nine," Maria replied. Then in a softer voice to Caden she said, "I've got to go."

He frowned, nodded and released her.

Caden looked out the window. A week of gentle snowfall had transformed the area into a carpet of white. The branches of evergreen trees sagged with snow. *A gentle snowfall. No, gentle isn't the word. Many people are still living in cars and tents.* Images of the FEMA camps covered in snow flashed through his mind. *This will only add to the misery of the destitute.*

He shuddered, tossed another log on the fire, and decided to put on a heavier shirt.

As he put on a flannel shirt from the closet, he heard the long heavy stride of his father come up the stairs and down the hall, then he heard Sue waddle along the hallway and down the creaking stairs.

A grumble from his stomach turned his mind to breakfast. He had thought about the food situation many times and never found an answer. *If everyone in the community shared all they had we would all starve before the next harvest. If we share a little we delay the inevitable. Many of the old and infirm are already dead. Those that don't have family, can't work or don't have useful skills will probably not survive the winter.*

He left his room and headed downstairs feeling guilty for not starving.

Caden followed the aroma into the dining area. Maria sat at a corner of the table with Adam on her lap. The rest of the family, except his father, were either seated or moving plates and bowls to the table. No one ate. Caden sat next to Maria. "Where's Dad?"

"He said he had to get something from the attic."

"Now?" Caden hoped he wouldn't be long.

One after another, everyone sat down. As a child, Caden had always thought of the dining table as huge, but this morning with five adults and a baby around it, and soon his father, it was full.

He glanced at Susan, wondered if she was lonely despite the full house, and pondered the fate of his brother in Seattle. *This year started with such promise. Peter was going…no is going to be a father. I had a new position with an up and coming Senator in the capital of the most powerful country on the planet. Such things are so easily stripped away.* He sighed out loud.

Maria squeezed his hand. "Don't worry about Hansen and

war today."

"Okay," he said as the sound of footsteps and thuds came from the stairwell.

His father entered the room carrying something vaguely familiar. Standing beside Maria he unfolded the wooden contraption.

Caden leaned back for a clearer view. "That old highchair was in the attic?"

His dad nodded. "There are a lot of interesting things up there. We've been bringing down the useful or tradable items."

Lisa looked at it askew. "I think I sat in that thing."

"You did and Peter and Caden." His mom grinned.

Trevor sat at the end of the table beside the highchair and smiled as Adam slapped the tray. Then he reached out and all the adults held hands around the table.

"Lord, bless this food and those around this table. We pray for Peter's safety..."

"Amen," Sue whispered.

"...and that our family and this community will be safe. We pray that there will be enough to eat in the coming months. And Lord, you told us to pray for our leaders and we do pray for them, but we also pray that you will save us from their foolishness. Amen."

That morning the family ate well from the bounty of their land.

After breakfast his dad said, "Dress warm and meet me in the barn. I'm working on a project and it'll go faster with two of us."

Caden had hoped to spend time with Maria. He shot her an apologetic glance and went to find his coat and gloves.

While pulling on his jacket, the hum of his phone vibrating on the nightstand distracted him. With one arm in the sleeve he looked at the display. Dr. Scott? He reached out his hand, paused and then answered the call.

"Good morning, Caden. How are you?"

"Great. I still have some bruises and a tender spot on the head, but no headaches. Is that why you called?"

"Well, no. I'm calling about Cruz."

Caden's gut tightened.

"There's no longer a medical reason to keep him in the hospital and, we need the room."

He knew this was coming, but didn't want to deal with it today, so he put the doctor off by saying, "I'll talk with the Sheriff about moving him to the jail. *Or just shooting him.*

Caden tried to put Cruz out of his mind as he walked downstairs. Sue sat by the fireplace reading a book on babies and childbirth. He paused, stoked the fire and added a log. His mom, Maria and Lisa talked and laughed in the kitchen. He was tempted to join them, if just for a moment, but he knew his father was waiting. Reluctantly he left and walked to the barn.

Along one wall was a stack of firewood. He paced off over twenty feet and nodded approvingly. *About three cord.*

As a child he had asked his father if he could help split the firewood. Caden couldn't remember exactly how old he was when his dad, after careful instruction, handed him the ax. Hours and blisters later they had a good supply of wood. His father 'volunteered' both him and Peter for firewood duty many times after that, but Caden never again asked for the opportunity.

Still, as he gazed at the large stack, the memory of blisters faded and a measure of reassurance filled him. Food and wood would get them through this winter.

Seeing his father step from the tack room, Caden said, "You've got a good stack of wood here."

"I think we have enough for the rest of this winter." His dad smiled at Caden. "Maria helped with a lot of that"

"Maria helped you cut and split three cords of wood?"

"She's not that good at splitting, but she's fine with a chainsaw."

Caden laughed.

"Follow me," his dad said. "I've got something to show you."

In a stall at the end of the barn was a pile of lumber and something covered by a blue tarp.

Pulling the tarp back, his dad revealed a pile of clear, plastic-like, material.

Caden knelt and inspected the sturdy, double layered, transparent sheets. "This stuff looks like plastic, but what is it?"

"The guy I got it from called it twin-wall polycarbonate."

"What are you going to do with it?"

"Remember the old greenhouse beside the garden?"

"That old thing? It's falling down."

Trevor grabbed a 2 by 4. "We're going to fix it up."

"Half the panes are...oh." He smiled looking at the polycarbonate sheets. "We're going to be out here for a while."

"Yeah." His dad handed him a tool belt. "Let's get started."

As they set the first new piece in place, Caden asked, "How did you get the materials?"

"We had a lot of wood up in the loft. The plastic stuff, well, that was expensive."

"How much?"

"The only thing he was willing to trade for was booze or coffee."

"We don't have much in the way of liquor."

"Now we don't have much in the way of coffee."

"You traded away the coffee?"

Trevor nodded.

Caden looked over the dilapidated building and wished he had a cup warming his fingers right then. He imagined drinking it and feeling it warm him from inside. He could almost smell the aroma. "This greenhouse better be worth it."

An hour later the two men had replaced a dozen 2x4s and nearly as many panes. *This is fixing up nice. We'll be starting tomatoes, squash and cucumbers in it soon.*

As he rested while his father cut another board, Caden counted the needed panels. "I think we could build two with what you have back in the barn."

"I could."

Caden was confused. "Why trade away the coffee for more than we need?"

His father grinned widely. "Any leftover is going to the church. They're building a community garden in the field behind the sanctuary."

"I've talked about finding and building greenhouses. I'm glad it is getting done."

His dad seemed less enthused. "It's a good idea, but learning the gardening or farming skills necessary to feed a family can take years."

Caden looked around. "I remember this place filled with

plants."

"Your mom and I grew up on farms and even so, there were years the crops failed."

Caden didn't want to imagine a crop failure this year. He picked up his pace. This building was going to give the Westmore clan the early start they needed for their garden.

Several hours later, Nikki barked repeatedly as a pickup rumbled down Hops Road.

Caden recognized the red Ford of his XO and, figuring he was coming to see Lisa, continued to nail a support beam into place.

A couple minutes later Brooks came around the barn, in uniform, carrying a black briefcase. Caden groaned. *This is no social call.*

Brooks greeted Trevor and then saluted Caden. "We need to talk—privately."

CHAPTER EIGHTEEN

Caden invited the XO into the tack room of the barn. A rusty woodstove stood in the corner. A dented blue enamel coffee pot sat on top. Caden picked it up hoping some coffee remained, but found only the dark residue of past brews.

When he was a teen the room held saddles, bridles, tack and grooming equipment. Now it was his father's man cave. Peg board lined the walls with tools neatly hung. A work bench ran along one side with drawers and toolboxes underneath. "What's up?" Caden asked.

Brooks set the briefcase on the bench and turned the dial on the combination. "A courier delivered an operations order and op plan this morning. I reviewed both and it was clear you needed to see it immediately." He handed him a folder, stamped SECRET in bold red letters.

Caden flipped open the file. "Give me the brief."

"It orders us to provide support for Operation Lexington against gangs and terrorists in the Renton, Burien, SeaTac, Kent, and Des Moines areas."

Caden laid the map out on the bench. The red blast area and yellow contaminated zone were clearly marked on it.

Brooks tapped his finger on a small rectangular area. "We'll be here, just outside of Renton, in Hillcrest.

The area was marked "Golf 181."

"We're directed to set up a Combat Support Hospital and logistic center at an abandoned office building." He pointed to another spot on the map. "The op plan says the goals are to restore law and order and to secure access to and operation of SeaTac airport on the southern edge of the yellow zone…"

Still staring at the message Caden said, "All of this is way out of our area of operations."

"…and control of regional port facilities."

"Uh huh," Caden said still focused on the message.

With concern in his voice Brooks said, "The port is still under the control of the People's Liberation Army."

Caden pursed his lips "Our part in this is minor." He remembered General Harwich saying the Chinese were using the flow of refugees, gangs and other criminals to expand their sphere of influence. "I see several Guard units, State Patrol and local law enforcement, but I don't see regular army units in or near our op area."

Caden rubbed his chin. "This message is vague about the Port of Tacoma portion of the op, but look at the units devoted to it." He moved his finger in an arc around the port. A dozen regular army units were deployed in that area.

"I saw that." Brooks brow furrowed.

"Pushing back against the Chinese zone of control was bound to happen when the new congress refused to ratify the friendship treaty."

Brooks' brow puckered deeper. "The PLA isn't going to just pack up and go home."

"There's no mention of taking the port from the Chinese Army. The operation may be against the gangs, and a show of force to prevent PLA expansion in this area." Caden leaned over the bench. "The only large operating airfield at the moment is Joint Base Lewis-McChord. Command would want to control the airports, but they don't mention the nearby King County Airport."

"It's just inside the red zone and…." Brooks tapped the spot on the map and slowly shook his head.

"What? Did something happen there?"

Thousands of people went to that airfield just after the blast. Since it was nearby and used by the aircraft factory and private pilots, it was as busy as SeaTac."

"That seems reasonable, go to the airfield until the fires burn out."

Brooks sighed. "The fires surrounded the field and burned for days."

107

"No one got out?"

He shook his head. "Heat, thirst, radiation. I never heard of anyone getting out alive."

"The bodies are still there?"

Brooks nodded. "It's in the red zone

The two men stared at the map. Caden finally broke the awkward silence. "This might be a plan to out maneuver the Chinese by seizing control of SeaTac before they do and confine the PLA to the port."

Brooks smiled weakly. "I'm sure a second airport would help with relief supplies, but...."

Caden shook his head. "There are two elements to this operation, and neither is about relief supplies. Even the name, Operation Lexington, hints at something larger. Of course command wants to restore order and they want to resume operations at SeaTac, but as soon as that is done, I think Monroe plans to push the Chinese out of the state."

Brooks rested his palm on the papers. "Why don't they say that in the message?"

"Maybe some units have been told, or will be, but we're just a rear support unit. There's no need to tell us much."

"They want us in place by 0500 Monday."

"I guess I'll be heading north in less than forty-eight hours."

"I should command this deployment. You should stay here in overall command of the armory and our area."

Caden placed his finger on the map. "For a normal support operation I would agree, but this could go badly and I've done urban combat maneuvers..."

"How do I get experience if I don't...?"

"...and our area includes the neighborhood where my brother lived. I want to check it out. If we were being sent to the area where your family lived, I'd find a way to include you."

Brooks shook his head. "The only family I had were my parents and they were in the Seattle red zone."

"I can get to my brother's house. I'd like to think he's been there, left a message, and maybe been sent somewhere else." He shrugged. "It's a small hope, but I need to follow up on it."

Brooks nodded. "I understand."

"I'll tell the sheriff that we are pulling most of our men up north for a few days. He won't be pleased."

"Maria really won't be pleased," Brooks said with a grimace.

Caden cringed. "I'm glad this is classified. The less she knows the better."

Brooks cast him a doubtful look.

"The Army is clearing out gangs and we are the backup. That's the brief, and that little should amount to an unclassified overview of our part of the op. Anyway, that's going to be my position with Maria—and the sheriff. Back me up on it, okay?"

"It is what the message says."

It is, but.... Caden shuddered inwardly at the thought of engaging units of the PLA, the world's largest army. "I should probably go tell Maria and the sheriff what I can."

"Before you go there's one more thing."

"About the op plan?"

"No. That kid you've been trying to help...."

Caden tensed. "Zach? What about him?"

"He told the First Sergeant that his mom is in the hospital and he needs a few days off."

"What happened to her?"

"The kid didn't say. I called the hospital, but they won't say anything either."

"That young man has more than his share of bad luck." Caden sighed deeply and looked out the window. "Give him whatever time he needs."

Brooks nodded. "I did." He returned the papers to the briefcase.

Stepping to the door of the tack room, Caden called for his father to take a break. "I have news to share with the family."

The three men walked toward the house in silence, but Brooks picked up his pace when Lisa stepped out on the porch.

Still deep in thought, Caden hardly glanced at his sister as he walked inside. He was just finishing his explanation when Brooks came in. Lisa was right behind him with a somber look on her face.

Maria, sitting next to him on the couch, asked the first question. "When will you be back?"

"I don't know for sure, but I think it will be days, not weeks."

Maria took his hand. "Where are you going?"

"North, but I'm not supposed to say exactly."

"The red zone?" his mother asked.

"No not there, but…."

"If you're going to be close to our house, could you see if Peter has been there," Sue whispered. "See if he might still be…." Tears rolled down her cheeks.

He wasn't supposed to say where he would be, but he nodded anyway.

Rarely had he seen his mother cry, but she now dabbed at tears.

Maria broke the awkward silence. "You said you're in a backup role. So you won't be involved in the fighting? You'll be safe?"

No. Hundreds of guys will have guns and be shooting at each other. He smiled. "We'll be fine. We're just supporting other troops. Nothing will happen."

*   *   *

The sheriff threw a file onto his desk.

Caden, in a brown winter jacket and jeans, stepped into the office. "What's the problem?"

Hoover spun around. "Oh…you. I've got to get the deputies to warn me when you come."

Caden chuckled. "Is this a bad time?"

"No…well, are there any good times now?"

"These are difficult times, but what do you mean exactly?"

Hoover plopped into the seat behind his desk. "Remember those people we arrested for breaking into the school greenhouse?"

Caden nodded.

"Well, they were lucky."

Caden's confusion must have shown.

"They're alive." The sheriff sighed. "Just after the attack on Seattle we had a rash of looting and justifiable homicides. I thought things were returning to normal, but this," he said pointing to the file on his desk, "is the fourth shooting death this week."

"Are they drug related?"

"In normal times a rash of shootings would probably be drug related, but most of the serious dopers are dead and the supply is drying up fast." The sheriff shook his head. "No, these are people getting shot stealing food or fighting over it." He stared into the distance. "It's going to get ugly if more food doesn't arrive."

Caden thought of Zach and how the boy managed to feed his family by fishing, hunting and working at the armory. He was proud of the young man. "Food distribution within the country has been disrupted by the attacks, and now the fighting, and not enough food aid is coming in. I think the situation will get worse before it gets better."

Hoover nodded. "That's what I'm thinking."

"I'm afraid I have more bad news for you."

The sheriff frowned.

He provided Hoover with the same unclassified brief he had given his family.

"When will you be back?"

Caden chuckled. "That was the first question Maria asked."

"But for different reasons."

"Thanks for the assurance," Caden grinned. "I don't know when I'll be back. Days, a couple of weeks…." He shrugged. "And I don't want to make your job tougher but…we need to discuss Cruz."

Hoover's eyes widened.

Caden relayed the conversation he had with the doctor earlier that morning.

The sheriff sighed. "You're just a bundle of joyful news this morning." He stared out the window for a moment. "Well, we could just…."

"We can't shoot him."

Hoover laughed. "How did you know I was thinking that?"

"Because when Scott told me we needed to move Cruz, shooting him was the first thought I had."

"He is at least an accomplice to murder and theft. Under the martial law edict you could issue…."

Caden held up his hand. "There are only thirty-eight hours before I have to leave and I've a lot to do. We'll deal with him when I get back."

The sheriff sighed. "Okay. The jail is overcrowded, but I'll find a cell for him. Can you leave a man or two to help with the move?"

Caden nodded. "Brooks will stay behind with a few of the newer men. They can help with the transfer."

As he stepped from the building, Caden basked in the warm winter sun. He looked north, toward Seattle. *The blast killed so many. It probably killed my brother, Peter.* A line of hills, covered in low gray clouds, stood between him and those blighted cities and towns. *Soon I'll be on the other side of those hills.*

As Caden continued to stare at the distant peaks, clouds obscured the sun leaving him in shadow. A cold breeze chilled him. Memories of battles, in Fallujah, Kamdesh, Hansen and more, flashed through his mind. *I thought it was over...behind me.* With a deep sigh, he flipped up his collar and headed toward the armory and the coming conflict.

CHAPTER NINETEEN

Maria sat beside him, as Caden drove to church.

"I feel bad about leaving Sue behind to watch the house," Maria said.

"She has Nikki to help her," Caden said with a grin. "Besides, she said she wanted to stay."

Maria nodded, but was clearly not satisfied.

Caden's thoughts drifted to the upcoming operation and battles of the recent past. *How many times have I had a gun pointed at me this year? How many times have I been shot at?*

Ahead the road curved up the slope, but between old apple trees Caden saw the white, wood-frame church that had dominated the hilltop for longer than he had lived.

I haven't been to church since the Battle of Olympia. I know Mom and Dad like it when I go, but life has been so busy. For several moments, images and emotions from the battle surged through him. He didn't like that the media included the fight at Hansen with the overall battle. The Hansen combat was referred to as a skirmish. Caden shook his head. The Hansen fight was small in comparison to the main battle around the capital and it was just a part of the overall conflict that day. Still, it seemed unfair to those who fought and died on both sides of the battle to call it a skirmish, but there was little he could do about it.

People riding horseback and walking in the street toward the church caused him to slow the car. More often now, people treated streets as wide paths and cars as intruders. He gave a horse plenty of space as he drove by. Farther ahead another horse pulled an ancient wagon slowly up the hill. Several kids jumped aboard as it passed.

Trees on the edge of the church parking lot served as hitching posts for horses. There were more cars on the lot than the last time he had been there, but parking was more than ample. Caden pulled into a spot that faced the large field behind the church.

A long Quonset-hut-style greenhouse dominated one side of the field. Two smaller backyard greenhouses stood alongside. A hill of black earth rose nearby and a chain-link fence would soon enclose the area. Several dozen raised-bed gardens were under construction. No one was there now, but clearly the field had been an area of intense activity.

Caden approached the largest greenhouse. A wooden door frame was at one end with hinges, but no door had yet been hung. PVC pipes about four feet apart arched like ribs from one side to the other. The entire structure was covered with heavy plastic sheeting. Even with one end open the air inside was warm. Benches lined the length. Narrow wooden tables with slats were designed for greenhouses, other tables were just available flat surfaces. Trays and pots in a multitude of shapes, sizes and material lined both sides.

At the sound of the church bell, Caden turned.

Maria stood just inside the structure watching him.

"I'm glad I saw all of this."

She nodded and reached out her hand. Together they walked back to the family.

The old horse-drawn wagon pulled in front of the church and children jumped from both sides.

As they entered the sanctuary, Caden's thoughts were on the greenhouses. Holding onto the image of those beside the church and the one on the family farm lifted his spirit. The structures seemed to say, 'We will survive this winter. We will be here next year.'

The church faced east and the morning light poured in through a large stained glass window casting the congregation in shades of red, green and blue. The sanctuary was largely full except for the first two rows. As the Westmore clan filed into a front row pew the congregation stood and sang, *It is Well With My Soul.*

Caden joined in.

The announcements were mostly about the coming planting. "If you have extra seeds please bring them to the exchange in room ten. Also, if you need seeds go there. You probably noticed the hill of black soil. The Grange is helping us organize and build a community garden beside the church. You can sign up for a plot...."

The government is fractured, the money nearly worthless, the economy is in a death spiral, but here there is hope. Caden smiled thinking of Zach and how he provided for his family and the way his dad found the materials to rebuild the decrepit greenhouse. *Yes, there is a future.*

He was lost in thought for several minutes and then his attention focused on the older, gray-haired man in a dark suit fervently speaking to the congregation. Caden recognized him as the pastor of the church.

He pointed at Caden and their eyes locked.

"Will you?" he asked.

In his confusion, Caden almost asked, "What?"

The pastor turned to the other side of the congregation. "Will you?" The elder's eyes swept the gathering. "Who will answer God's call in Ezekiel and stand in the gap on behalf of the land?"

Relieved that he wasn't being personally asked, Caden dwelled on the question. *This town is lucky to have men like Hoover and my father. During the chaos of the terror attacks, they saved Hansen. Governor Monroe is struggling to save the state and maybe the country. They are standing in the gap.*

The pastor lifted his arms. "Rise up, followers of the Lord, and strengthen what remains before all is lost."

*   *   *

Caden stopped by the hospital later that day, in uniform. Even though Zach was not a soldier, he considered this part of his trip an official duty. The last couple of weeks he had performed well at the armory and earned the respect of the First Sergeant. Not an easy task.

He wanted to check on the young man, and his mother, and see if he could help.

After minutes of weaving down identical halls he came to her room. The mother and two teenage girls were inside. Caden recognized the redheaded teen as Vicki, Zach's sister. She sat in the corner swaying to music only she could hear on her earbuds and writing in a notebook.

He thought the other girl with blonde hair, was the one he had seen with Zach at the library market. She was pretty, with well-manicured nails, new jeans and a lacy yellow blouse, but right now, that was off-set by her snoring.

Caden stepped into the room

Vicki swung to her right, saw Caden and gasped. Pulling the earbuds from her ears she said, "I didn't know you were there."

"Sorry I startled you."

The blonde stretched and then went wide-eyed at the man in the room.

"I'm just checking on Zach and your family."

"Mom is…well the doctor won't say, but I don't think they believe she will ever wake up."

"Was it a stroke or…." It was a natural question, but Caden immediately felt nosy and regretted asking.

Vicki's head hung low.

"It was Bo," the blonde said.

"What?" Caden asked.

With a big sigh Vicki said, "I think we need help. Zach needs help. I'm afraid he's going to do something bad."

Caden sat down. "Tell me everything and I'll see what I can do."

More sighs and looks passed between the girls.

"You need to tell him," the blonde said.

Vicki nodded. "This guy Bo, gave Mom booze and she drank it," she shook her head, "like a fish. I think he liked Mom to begin with, but then he was just using her to get to Zach."

He looked at her doubtfully.

"Yeah, he wants Zach to steal things from the armory," the blonde agreed.

"Steal what, exactly."

Hands weaving in the air as if drawing, Vicki said, "Guns, bullets and parts of them, you know like the things the bullets go in."

"Magazines?" Caden asked.

"Yeah, I guess that's what it's called. But Zach wouldn't do it."

"Good," Caden said.

"But then Bo gave Mom drugs. I think Bo wanted to get her hooked so he'd have more power over Zach, and Mom too, maybe."

Gesturing toward the mother, Caden asked, "Was this an overdose?"

"Kinda…ah…Mom…she tried to kill herself." The girl stared at the floor for a moment. "And Zach said he was going to kill Bo. Can you stop my brother before…?"

"Is Bo a nickname? Do you know his full name?"

"Ah…I think Bo is his real name. I've heard his last name but…."

"Robert Bo Hendricks," the blonde said.

"How did you know that, Delynn?" Vicki asked.

The girl blushed "Bo's creepy. When he first started visiting your house, I asked my dad to check on him." She looked at Caden. "My dad's a lawyer." Turning back to Vicki she said, "Dad didn't care for Zach before, but what he found out about Bo really turned him against…well, all of you. I'm sorry."

Vicki hugged Delynn but looked at Caden. "Can you arrest him?

Caden looked at his watch and silently cursed his lack of time. In less than fifteen hours he would lead most of his men north in Operation Lexington. "I will do everything I can. If you see Zach, tell him to go to the armory."

The girls smiled and nodded.

Caden wasn't hopeful as he left the room. In addition to his lack of time, Bo would probably deny everything Zach and Vicki accused him of doing. *A classic they said, he said.*

Still considering what to do, he continued down a long straight hallway toward the other end of the building and the less noble reason for his visit to the hospital. He told Brooks and his family that he would visit Zach and his mother before he left, but he told no one that he also wanted to see Cruz.

He didn't know exactly why he needed to see the prisoner. Perhaps it was just to assure himself that the murderer was there and would remain in custody. Caden didn't plan to say anything to him. Oh, he did want to gloat that MS-13 and the other gangs were about to be destroyed. But he wouldn't. The less Cruz knew the better. However, he could stand there, look the thug in the eye and know that he would never breathe free air again and his gang, at least in this area, would soon be decimated.

As he walked down the hall, Caden smiled. That would be enough.

But when Caden arrived at the room where the interrogation had occurred, three patients occupied the space and none of them was Cruz.

He asked about the former occupant, but they knew nothing. Caden left and found a nurse.

"That awful man," she said with a visible shudder. "The sheriff had him moved to a more secure place in the hospital a couple of days ago." She gave him directions.

Caden turned down one bland pastel colored passage and then another. He waved to Dr. Winfield, turned down another corridor and soon saw a deputy seated beside a door.

The lawman stood as Caden approached.

"I need to see the prisoner." He felt his face warm. There was no need. This was a want, an emotional desire to look into the face of the man who had killed one of his men, and tried to kill him. Caden had a need for Cruz to know who was in control.

The deputy unlocked the door and Caden stepped into a tiny windowless room. He wondered if it had been a storage area before it was a prison cell.

The space was empty except for a chair, table and hospital bed. The bed was bolted to the floor as far from the door as possible and Cruz was handcuffed to it.

Just inside, Caden stared at the thug.

Slowly Cruz opened his eyes. "You're disturbing my beauty rest soldier boy."

Caden remained silent wondering if he should convene a tribunal and dispose of Cruz. Thinking about that and the upcoming operation to destroy MS-13 and the other gangs brought a grin to Caden's face.

"What you smiling about?"

Caden had what he wanted. *I'll wait till I return to decide Cruz's fate.* He looked around the small space. "Do you like your room?"

Cruz cursed.

"I think you'll like your next room even less."

"You moving me or you gonna try and kill me?"

Again Caden smiled. "For now I think mov…." He had said more than he planned, more than he should. Turning away, he banged on the door.

The deputy let him out.

In the hall Caden wondered if the little he said was too much. The criminal had to know that he would be moved to a jail, but Caden had confirmed it. Still he didn't know a day or time.

Caden turned to the deputy. "Does Cruz have any visitors?"

"Yes, a teenage girl. She says she's his sister."

"How do you know?"

He shrugged. "I don't know, but prisoners can have visitors."

Caden looked skeptical. "Do you have a visitor log?"

The officer retrieved a green journal from a nearby drawer. It showed a 'Carina Cruz' visiting every other day.

"What can she do?" the deputy asked. "A nurse searches her going in and out and we have a monitor on the room."

"I don't know," Caden said as he walked away. As he left the hospital, Caden looked at the refugees along the edge of the parking lot and wondered how many were in town. *Are any of them gang members? How many are friends of Cruz?* He sighed. *I'll be glad when he's in jail.* Caden rubbed his chin. *Hoover should know this Bo character.* He would stop by the sheriff's office and tell him what he'd learned this morning. *Even if I don't have enough evidence to convict Bo, I'm going to issue an arrest order. It may stop Zach from doing something stupid.*

CHAPTER TWENTY

Monday morning was hours away—and there was no coffee. Caden sighed and then said his goodbyes to both his mom and dad. Looking at them, standing in robes and old slippers, he said, "You didn't have to see me off."

"Yes we did," his mother said.

After hugging her, Caden joined Maria and Lisa near the front door. They were about to leave when he heard the slow waddle of Sue as she came down the creaky stairs.

Caden walked over and hugged her. "You shouldn't have gotten up."

"I had to." Sue handed him several sheets of folded paper. "It's our home address, in Kent, a map of the neighborhood, the address of the police station, everything I could think of. Please find him or...well, I've got to know." Tears rolled down her cheeks.

He wasn't sure how long he embraced her.

As they walked out onto the porch Maria said, "I'll drive."

Caden, carrying his helmet in one hand and adjusting his holster with the other, did not object.

Lisa rode along in the backseat.

Caden wasn't sure why an uneasy silence hung over the car. Perhaps they were all tired, or were focused on private thoughts. He didn't know, but the quiet remained unbroken.

When they rounded the final curve to the armory, every light seemed to be on. Truck engines roared and a hundred men scurried about the post. Some loaded supplies into every available vehicle, others seemed to be part of choreographed chaos.

"I thought this operation was a secret," Lisa said.

"We could have been quieter, but the homes around here

would have still heard us and the whole operation is going to begin, ah…" Caden looked at his watch, "soon."

The guard waved Maria past. She pulled into the lot and parked in Caden's spot, beside Brooks' pickup.

Lisa jumped out and trotted toward the building.

Maria smiled in her direction and then looked at Caden with a serious expression. "I'm glad Brooks isn't going with you. I like Lisa, and don't want to see her hurt if something happened to him."

"Nothing is going to happen to me."

"You can't promise that."

"We are only supporting…."

Maria shook her head. "I've never had much to do with the military, but this feels bigger than supplies and medicine."

He pursed his lips and tried to figure out what he could say that wasn't classified. "Our orders are to support other units." He didn't want to leave her this way, but it was all he could say.

Maria stared at him with sad eyes and then pulled him toward her and kissed him.

Caden grinned. "I'll be back soon—for more of that. He put his helmet on and headed toward the building.

The numerous lights around the armory blocked his view of most stars, but the sky appeared clear. A chill in the air prompted him to zip up his jacket. He looked for Brooks, but found Lisa sitting in the office looking bored.

"He's on that big lawn to the north of the building."

"Parade ground."

"What?"

"It's called a parade ground."

"Do you parade around on it?"

"Sort of. It's an old military term."

She shrugged.

With a handful of papers, the XO stood on the edge of the grass with First Sergeant Fletcher. Brooks talked while pointing at different trucks. "Oh, I didn't see you," he said when Caden was beside him. "Here is the roster and supply list. Eighty men leave with you. I'll keep ten here with me. MOPP gear has been issued, but winds are to the east away from your area, so there should be no new fallout. The squad leaders have done the pre-combat inspection."

Caden flipped through the pages. "Good job XO. Assemble the men. I want to address them before we leave."

Brooks notified Fletcher and soon the men formed ranks on the parade ground. When they were ready, First Sergeant Fletcher called, "Company!"

The Platoon Sergeants called, "Platoon!"

As Fletcher called the men to attention, Caden came out of the shadows.

The two saluted and then Caden waited for everyone to jog to their final places.

"At ease." Caden scanned the assembled soldiers. In the rear, at the edge of the shadows, he noticed both Maria and Lisa. He sighed, not wanting them to hear now, what he wouldn't say earlier to the whole family.

Family. Even though they weren't married, in his mind he included Maria in that statement. *It is the way I think of her.*

Caden smiled at her, even though she wouldn't see it from across the parade ground. He chose his words carefully, knowing Maria, and through her, the rest of the family, would hear what he was about to say.

"As you know, we have been ordered to provide logistics and medical support for units engaging gang and other criminals in and around the southern portion of the yellow zone. At this time I do not expect that we will see combat, but I cannot, will not, rule it out.

"We serve a troubled, divided nation and many are seeking to take advantage of our time of need. All of us must be ready for whatever may come. Focus on your duties, be aware of your surroundings and anticipate what might go wrong. That way you come home on your feet, instead of on your back in a body bag." He slowly looked over the men. Maria and Lisa still stood at the edge of the grass. He hoped his words reassured both them and the soldiers. "Mount up."

Before they headed north, Caden sought out Maria. Taking her hand when he found her, he said, "I feared you might have left."

She gave him a knowing grin. "I thought you were only supporting the operation."

"We are."

She shook her head. "That wasn't what you were preparing

the men for."

He took in a deep breath and let it out slowly. "No, it wasn't. What I told you was the truth of my orders, but I've learned...well, sometimes words conceal as much as they reveal. I hope I'm wrong."

She stepped close and pulled him closer. Speaking just inches from his lips she said, "Don't be afraid to tell me what you're thinking. The truth from you protects me more than a lie or silence ever could."

She kissed him. "Stay safe."

"Yes, to everything you said." He smiled. "And you stay safe too."

"Me? The Westmore farmhouse is the safest home for a hundred miles."

*   *   *

Nearly an hour later as the convoy rolled along highway 12 on its way out of Hansen, Caden thought about his conversation with Maria. He hadn't told her about the operation, but she had figured out enough and, in the process, he was reminded of her strength.

He caught a glimpse of movement in the stream along the highway. *It must be Zach and his sister.* But, as he passed he thought he saw two girls. *Vicki, and the other girl I met yesterday?* He shrugged. *Doubtful, she seemed a little too posh for waders, fish and mud.*

He looked to the other side of the road and, through the trees, glimpsed light from home.

The convoy rumbled along for several miles. Ahead a lighted sign outside the church by the freeway caught his attention. He had been reunited with Sue there and fought a gunfight in the lobby, but he never knew the name of the church. Now, for the first time since he returned home, the sign blazed in digital colors, 'Welcome to Zion Church.'

His eyes lingered on the sign as the driver turned onto the freeway. *It's another hopeful indication that life is returning to normal.*

They drove north along a nearly deserted freeway, through a quiet, but well lit, Olympia. Every light seemed to be on at Lewis-McCord, but as they continued north out of Tacoma the suburbs turned dark.

At the end of a two hour drive they arrived at a five-story brick medical building surrounded on three sides by a large parking lot. Smaller professional buildings, shops and offices lined the edges. On the opposite side of the street was another parking lot with flanking apartment buildings and a smattering of fir and maple trees.

Caden set the map on his lap and spoke into the radio. "This is the location, First Sergeant." When his vehicle pulled to a stop, Caden jumped out, eager to stretch his legs. Fletcher deployed the men to secure the perimeter.

The faint smell of smoke hung in the air. The glass in the door of the medical building had been broken, along with several nearby windows. More than a dozen cars dotted the parking lot. Some were stripped of parts, some were burned out hulks, but a few were nice and intact, as if waiting for their owner's return.

They were only a half-mile from the freeway, close enough to hear traffic during a normal rush hour, but the world this day was silent. Sunlight peeked between nearby towers casting an early morning glow between dark shadows.

Caden walked over to Fletcher. "The place looks nice."

"Yeah, if you like eerily quiet and deserted cities." He shook his head. "I'm waiting for a horde of zombies to pour across the parking lot."

"Well, if they do First Sergeant, let's be ready."

"Yes, sir."

Caden pointed to the central structure. "Have some soldiers search it."

He nodded. "Already done. They're checking all the rooms and will set up an observation post on the roof." Fletcher pointed to three nearby buildings. "Men will setup in those places also."

"Has anyone checked for radiation yet?"

"The medic said, 'don't buy a home here.' The air is clear, but he's already found several hot spots."

A cold wind blew across the lot.

"It's from the east." Caden said flatly. "We're okay."

"Yes, but when the winds blow from the north...?"

He nodded. "Set up hourly checks for radiation. If the readings climb, let me know immediately.

Satisfied that Fletcher was securing the perimeter, Caden walked to the main building and carefully stepped through the shattered door glass.

Inside the powerless building, deep shadows hid much of the entrance. The smell of death hung heavy in the air. He pulled out his flashlight and swept the dark corners just inside. Within moments the beam found a badly decayed body slumped across a seat in the corner. The stench moved him onward.

Beyond the lobby two medics, and several other soldiers, were dividing up the building for a thorough search.

Caden continued on. The structure was designed for doctors of various specialties. Each had a separate lobby, exam rooms, administrative and doctor offices and all were colored in various pastel shades. It would now serve as a forward medical and logistics center.

A sign on the wall pointed to a pharmacy. *I need to make sure that is secure.* He walked along a dark hallway, past stairs and useless elevators.

As he neared, the foul odor of death once again greeted him. Two large metal doors once secured the room, now they hung broken and open. Inside was a waiting area with a large counter. Behind it were the typical white shelves and myriad of bottles. Pills, bottles and broken glass littered the floor.

Peering over the counter, he spotted the body on the floor. He figured that all the narcotics had either been removed when the doctors evacuated or had been stolen afterwards, but he couldn't be sure.

He called over the radio to Fletcher and reported the bodies. "I need someone to secure the pharmacy doors. I want only the medics inside for now."

"Yes, sir. I'll get someone on it."

Caden continued up the stairs, inspecting rooms and talking with most soldiers. Nearly an hour later he reached the fourth floor.

Again he encountered one of the medics. "What have you got to report, Sergeant?"

"We've found fourteen bodies in the building. It looks like three died of gunshot wounds. The other eleven were located in a makeshift morgue. They were all radioactive and probably died of acute radiation sickness. We've started removing them. Later we'll dig a mass grave in one of the grassy areas at the edge of the parking lot."

"Good job." There was nothing more for Caden to do there

so he continued on, inspected the fifth floor and then went to the roof.

Exiting to the flat top of the building, he had a clear view of the surrounding area. He shook his head in dismay at the once proud cities of the Seattle metro area. A tall structure about three miles west burned like a torch. Smoke from smaller fires dotted the view. To the north the hills were scorched black by the wildfire after the blast. Looking through binoculars, Caden saw streaks of gray ash and brown mingled in the dead black earth. But it was the quiet that struck Caden. There was no pulse of human activity. The streets did not flow like arteries this way and that. All was stillness and silence. Caden recalled the cliché, 'quiet as the grave.' It was appropriate. The only sound was the rustle of the breeze in his ears. Finally, in the distance, a crow squawked.

A nearby soldier pointed. "Is that a pack of wild dogs?"

Using his binoculars, Caden quickly found the brown, slender animals with pointed ears and bushy tails." No, those are coyotes."

"Really? I grew up not far from here. I never saw wild animals running down the street."

"This isn't the metro area you grew up in anymore. *And it may never be again.* He walked along the parapet of the roof watching the pack until they were out of sight.

A lone dog barked.

Standing at the ledge he took in the full sweep of the view, abandoned cars, fire and smoke, the silence broken only by the wind or an occasional bird or dog. Seattle was gone or uninhabitable. The surrounding communities were dying flesh clinging to a corpse.

Clanging from the stairwell announced the arrival of the radio operator. Caden grabbed a bag of equipment from him and moved it a shady spot while the specialist went back for the antenna and cable. When he returned, Caden said, "As soon as you're setup, notify command that we're in position."

In the distance a woman screamed.

Caden wondered if the woman and the coyotes had found each other. He shook his head. The animals had been on the edge of the parking lot and the scream seemed distant and from the wrong direction.

Vehicles engines thundered.

A single shot crackled in the air.
The woman screamed again.

CHAPTER TWENTY ONE

Sporadic gunfire mixed with screams echoed off nearby glass and steel buildings.

The men on either side of Caden looked through binoculars, talked and pointed.

Gesturing toward the burning tower one private said, "It's hard to see that way with all the smoke."

Caden slid along the ledge. *The first crack of gunfire came from the south.* When he thought he was looking in the right direction there were too many shots, too much echo, and too much talking to figure a bearing. "Quiet everyone," he ordered. "If you actually see something or *know* where a shot came from report it, otherwise look and listen." Pointing to the man closest to him he said, "You stay with me on the south side. Sergeant, station the others on each side of the roof. Let me know if anything approaches our position." *Gunfire, a great start to the day.*

Clutching his radio he called, "Fletcher, do we have units in the buildings at the edge of the parking lot?"

"On the east and west, that's a roger. No contact reported at this time. I'm working on getting soldiers on the north and south."

Frustrated, Caden replied, "I think the shooting is coming from the south."

"Roger, I concur, we're crossing the parking lot now."

From atop the building he looked down as Fletcher led eight soldiers in a sprint across the asphalt. Caden turned to the man at his side. "If they come under fire, provide cover."

In seconds the nine reached a building on the far side and broke open a door.

Caden relaxed a bit as the men disappeared inside, but smoke continued to obscure his view and annoy his nose as he scanned the city beyond. He struggled to follow the vehicles by their sound. *The rate of gunfire accompanying the cars suggests they are firing at something, but what?*

Fletcher's voice came over the radio. "We see six to eight males in three civilian vehicles. They're firing at something forward of their position—buildings, cars…who knows."

"Roger that," Caden said. "I heard screams. Do you see a female?"

"Negative…no, wait…roger, two people are running toward our position."

Caden moved along the roof until he saw down the street. In the morning shadows it was difficult to see detail. He couldn't be sure of gender, but they held hands as they ran. Farther up the road a car turned the corner and headed toward them. A passenger hung out the window firing a pistol.

One of the runners fell.

The other knelt beside.

The two struggled to stand.

"Fletcher, this is Westmore. Provide cover fire."

Gunfire poured down the street.

The two runners huddled against the building. Then they seemed to realize they weren't being fired upon and together hobbled on towards Fletcher's position.

Burning rubber on the pavement the car retreated down the street, spun around the corner, and disappeared.

"We have the runners," Fletcher announced over the radio. "One is injured. I'll bring them to the main building. Have a medic standing by."

With one last look across the now quiet city, Caden headed down the dark stairwell. While on the first flight, the lights flickered and then came on.

From far below someone shouted, "Thank God for electricity!"

Amen. The engineers must have hooked up the generator. Caden exited the now well-lit stairwell and headed toward the elevators along a hallway that was a hive of activity with soldiers moving boxes, cleaning rooms or setting up gear.

A tapping sound filled the air. "Ah...is this thing on?"

Caden looked up at the speakers of the now working PA system.

"Ah we've got the lights on...you know that, but most other things aren't working yet, like the heat and elevators. Ah...that is all."

Within sight of his destination Caden did an about face and walked back to the stairs. *At least I'm going down.*

Near the bottom he met two soldiers carrying a body bag. He followed them down the last flight of stairs and into the lobby.

As the two men carried out the body, Fletcher and others arrived. With them were two gaunt and dirty teenage girls. The eyes of the girls followed the body bag out the door.

One of the teens had a bandage around her right leg and was supported by the other.

Two medics came from behind Caden.

The eyes of the girls fixed on the approaching soldier and they cringed.

Fletcher whispered to Caden. "They wouldn't let us touch them."

Caden looked around the lobby. A dozen men with guns stood with two traumatized girls. "I saw a female medic arrive earlier. Get her."

Minutes later, the woman medic helped the wounded girl onto a stretcher.

"Are you two sisters?" the medic asked softly.

Still holding hands, they both nodded.

"If you let go of your sister, I think we can fix you up in that room right over there." She gestured with her head and then looked at the other. "You can wait just outside."

The stretcher was carried into a nearby exam room.

Fletcher motioned for the other girl to follow him as he walked to Caden.

"This is the man I told you about. His name is Major Westmore."

She looks a year or so younger than Vicki and DeLynn, but that might be because she is half starved. "Call me Caden."

The girl's eyes drifted to the exam room.

"Would you like some food?"

She nodded and for the first time looked him in the eye.

A soldier brought an MRE.

The teen devoured it and then used her dirty fingers to get the last.

When she finished, Caden's stomach growled, and he realized he hadn't eaten since breakfast. *I should have asked for two.*

Once again, the girl looked toward the exam room.

"What's your sister's name?" Caden asked. "What's your name?"

"She's Beth. I'm Amy."

"Where are your parents, Amy?"

For several moments she was silent. Tears streaked her cheeks. "Dead."

Her tears had led him to that conclusion already, but he was surprised by the word. "When?"

"A couple of weeks ago."

Caden took a deep breath and let it out slowly. "It would help if you told me why you stayed in this area and about the guys who shot at you."

Amy's eyes drifted to the exam room door, and back to her feet. "Our car wouldn't work after the bomb went off. No cars worked. My dad had a shotgun and a pistol, so we stayed in the house for over a week. We didn't have much food or water, but we stayed. Then the fire came and we had to leave."

Amy sighed and for several moments was silent.

Caden was about to say they could talk later, when she spoke.

"Dad protected us—for a while." Tears ran down her cheeks. "They call themselves the 15th Street Gang. They shot Dad and then Mom. Then they took us and...." Her eyes closed.

"I understand. How did you know to come here?"

"They talked about soldiers moving into this building. They plan to leave. When I got the chance, I grabbed Beth and ran."

Smiling, Beth hobbled from the exam room on a crutch. One leg was clean and bandaged.

Caden decided to suspend the interview. He pointed to the medic. "I'll have her get both of you cleaned up and settled."

"Can my sister get some food?"

"Yes, I'll make sure she does."

Caden looked for the first sergeant and found him helping to unload medical supplies.

As he neared the group Caden said to Fletcher, "Walk with me."

The two men crossed the parking lot to the grassy strip and smaller buildings along the edge. "This is what worries me." He pointed to the wide access roads and green lawn. "If we're attacked, this is the way they will come."

"You don't expect the guys we encountered today to do anything like that do you? They'd get caught in a cross fire." Fletcher pointed at several nearby buildings where soldiers were stationed.

"From what Amy told me those thugs are leaving the area, but others might do something stupid. Our job is to establish this logistics center. Let's try to keep them outside of the perimeter."

Fletcher nodded. "We can use abandoned cars and sandbags to block access, but it will take at least a day to secure the entire area. Do you expect any trouble tonight?"

He shrugged. "Probably not tonight. But we were told to expect gang and criminal activity and, from what the teen told me, that is what we're dealing with."

Fletcher nodded agreement. "Those guys stay up late and sleep in, but I'll make sure we're prepared for them if they come this way again."

"We should be ready for anything." Caden smiled. "Even the zombie horde you were talking about."

"Also, keep a squad ready for quick reaction. If something happens I can take them and…."

"I should lead them, Sir."

Caden frowned. He had been a lieutenant when he left the service and lieutenants lead soldiers in combat, but Governor Monroe had promoted him when he took this job. He was a major and the senior officer on site. "Yes, First Sergeant, you'll lead them."

"I'll get on it."

Over the next few hours, the soldiers cleared abandoned cars from the parking lot and used them to form part of the defensive perimeter. The first supply convoy brought more soldiers and another generator. The two provided enough power for all the buildings.

Later convoys brought more medical equipment, fuel, food and other supplies. A triage area, surgical rooms and mess area were established in the main structure.

As the sun slid below the western buildings, Caden set out to inspect the work of the day. Even as he walked along the southern perimeter talking to sentries and inspecting barriers, more trucks arrived. Two were marked with red crosses. More soldiers jumped from the back of a third. Men unloaded crates from another.

By the time Caden had inspected the eastern and northern defenses, all that remained of the sun was a fading orange glow. A whirling sound caught his attention and he watched as a drone launched into the air. *Clearly this base is growing larger than our orders implied.*

He glanced at his watch. *Nearly seven.* Returning his gaze to the drone as it disappeared into the darkness, he concluded it had been a good day, but wondered about the night.

Turning back toward the main building, he pondered what next needed his attention. His stomach growled. *I missed chow.* He headed toward the conference room that had been transformed into the mess hoping there was at least an MRE available.

At the far end of the room a dozen soldiers clustered around a few tables. An older man stood at one end talking.

Caden spotted a cross on his uniform. *I didn't realize a chaplain had arrived.* He paused and listened.

"…book of Nehemiah, in the Old Testament, the walls of Jerusalem had been destroyed by war. Nehemiah returns to the city of his ancestors to restore what has been destroyed. We are like that."

"We're not building anything," a young soldier said.

"In the literal sense, no not yet, but I am certain that time will come. The terrorists tore down several of our great cities and now we're here, at the edge of one of them, to begin restoring what has been lost. When you're standing guard as a sentry out on the perimeter, you're like Nehemiah on the wall. Behind you is justice, order and democracy, and in front of you, what you keep out, is the enemy—ignorance, tyranny and chaos."

As the chaplain continued Caden glanced around for an MRE or even an apple. Then his radio squawked. "Westmore, this is Fletcher. Sentries report gunfire."

Food will have to wait. He was glad for the elevator that took him to the makeshift command center on the top floor. The pastel pink room was the office next to the stairwell. Cables ran from it to antennas on the roof. Filing cabinets lined up along the windows provided protection from gunfire. In the center stood a large table with a map of the area spread on it. On the far side a soldier flew one of the drones. Nearer to the door, Fletcher stood beside the radio operator which, at the moment, was silent.

"What's the brief, First Sergeant?"

"The gunfire is from the south but distant. None of the lookouts have seen any flashes. One drone is headed toward the convoy. I've order the launch of the second one to recon this area."

Caden relaxed a bit and sat at the table. His stomach rumbled loudly.

"Did you miss chow, Sir?" Fletcher asked.

He smiled. "Perhaps I should get some food." Caden headed for the door when a voice near panic came across the radio.

"Golf 181, this is army convoy south of your position at Fourth and Evergreen. We're blocked and taking fire from all sides. Request immediate assistance. Over."

Before the man stopped talking, Caden found their location on the map.

"Shall I head out with the ready squad?" Fletcher asked.

"We don't know what you're heading into. Take two squads and get the sergeants to ready all the men, including the new arrivals. I'll tell the convoy you're coming."

Fletcher hurried from the room as Caden radioed the unit under attack. His stomach grumbled again.

Caden went up to the roof and watched as four Humvees with M2s mounted on top rumbled across the parking lot and down the dark street. He turned as a whirl came from the other side of the building and watched the second drone climb into the night sky.

Observing the defenses, Caden walked along the edge of the roof. Below a squad with M4s trotted toward the perimeter.

Holding his radio he said, "Sentries, this is Westmore, report."

One after another they informed him of distant gunfire, but otherwise all was quiet.

Why would a gang attack an army convoy? Something isn't right here. Troubled, he returned to the command post.

The drone was still en route, but Caden was drawn to the video screen. The thermal black and white image displayed buildings in ghostly gray. The unused roads appeared black.

When the craft was over the battle, fighters showed as white figures moving across a black and gray background. Gunfire appeared as flashes on the screen.

Rarely had Caden viewed battle from this perspective and never with his own soldiers.

The radio crackled as the Humvees approached.

"Convoy this is Golf 181 coming in from the north."

"Golf 181 this is Convoy. Roger. We have shooters south of you in the two buildings on the north corner of Evergreen and Fourth Avenue."

"I sure wish this drone was armed." Caden leaned over the shoulder of the pilot. "Swing around so we can see those buildings."

"Base and Convoy this is Golf 181. We have engaged the enemy."

CHAPTER TWENTY TWO

As the drone maneuvered toward the south side of the buildings, Caden relayed the positions of every shooter he spotted.

For the next ten minutes gunfire rattled across the radio from both the convoy and his men.

Breathe, remember to breathe. Listening to my people in combat is worse than actually being there.

"Convoy this is Golf 181. Route is clear ahead. Go!"

"Base this is Convoy. Need medics upon arrival."

Using his handheld radio, Caden informed the medics of incoming wounded, and then returned his concentration to the video display. When Fletcher reported that they had disengaged and were providing a rear guard, Caden sighed deeply. He stayed in the command post until the units were near and then ran to the elevator, punched the button and, when the doors didn't immediately open, hurried down the stairs.

Medics stood ready at the front of the building as Caden paced along the curb. Finally he heard Fletcher respond to the sentry's radio challenge.

Caden stood nearly at attention as the headlights appeared at the edge of the base.

Five trucks and two Humvees rumbled to a stop near him. Soldiers poured out. A young lieutenant followed several soldiers as they carried stretchers. The medics examined the wounded and ushered them inside. The remaining soldiers collected around the vehicles.

Walking among the people and trucks, Caden looked for the first sergeant. Then he heard approaching vehicles and counted four Humvees racing across the lot. As they pulled up and men climbed out, he saw familiar faces. "Good job! Well done."

Fletcher appeared from between two trucks with a cluster of soldiers behind. Several were bandaged, but walking. As soon as the first sergeant was in earshot Caden asked, "Did we lose anyone?"

The first sergeant shook his head. "The convoy had a few causalities, but we didn't lose any. Three injured, but they'll live." Fletcher retrieved a rifle from one of the men. "I got something for you, sir."

After looking over it closely, Caden nodded. "Type 56 variant of the AK-47."

"What does that mean?" A private asked.

Fletcher gritted his teeth. "It means it's made by the Chinese."

*   *   *

The morning after the skirmish, Caden awoke to the racket of a helicopter landing near the building. Within moments Fletcher was at the door of Caden's lavender blue office that, with a cot in the corner, also served as his bedroom.

"General Harwich, two other officers and a civilian bigwig just arrived on the chopper."

Caden rubbed his face. "When did you know they were coming?"

"About two minutes after the helo requested permission to land."

Caden dressed quickly and hurried out of the building with Fletcher.

In the pre-dawn darkness, three men in uniform stood together on the asphalt as the blades of the helicopter slowed. As salutes were exchanged the fourth man, in a business suit, turned. "David! The last time I saw you a Chinese soldier had messed up that pretty face of yours."

He cringed. "Yeah, that plan didn't go exactly the way I thought it would."

"Why are you here?"

"Governor Monroe asked me to accompany General Harwich on an inspection tour of the units."

"Well this is only the second day, but I'd be happy to show you what we've accomplished."

"We will get to that," The general interrupted. "I'm sure you've done well, but frankly Major, we have other business to conduct with you."

"Oh?"

"Where can we talk privately?"

"There's a conference room we can use." Caden turned to Fletcher. "Get the rifle you recovered and join us there."

The four men followed Caden into the main building. As soon as the door shut, the general asked about the fight the evening before.

"First Sergeant Fletcher led the men. He should provide details. From watching the drone and hearing his report, I can tell you whoever the attackers were they stood their ground under fire and fought like professionals. Several died rather than retreat."

Everyone was still talking when Fletcher returned.

"It appears the Chinese are providing first rate training and equipment." Caden passed the rifle to the general. "We took this during the fight."

One of the men with the general, an Army captain, shook his head. "The PRC government denies supplying weapons."

Caden gritted his teeth. "How can the Chinese government say that?" He tapped the rifle. "This was made in their country."

"That AK-47 variant has seen action in a dozen wars that I can think of, and is common in much of the world and the United States," the captain said. "How would you prove they supplied that rifle to Jihadists in the United States?"

Caden struggled to remain calm. "But we both know they did. Ah…did you say Jihadists?"

"The captain is merely paraphrasing what the PRC has said about the weapons," the general said. "Let's sit and discuss this over coffee."

"We haven't had any for more than a week."

The general nodded to a young lieutenant who pulled a 12 ounce bag of the brew from his briefcase.

"We're going to be here for a while," Harwich said to Caden. "Could you find a coffee pot and get some of this perked?"

Caden grinned. "Yes sir, I think we can do that."

For the next several minutes the war was put on hold as the

necessary hardware was found.

While the junior person in the room made coffee, one of the lieutenants unfolded a map on the table.

General Harwich looked at the chart, then at Caden. "Now that this combat support hospital and logistic center is established, and we know the lawless elements are nearby, we're going to move another unit in and put your soldiers in a forward position."

"Yes sir, but if I may ask, why us?"

"Your people have a reputation for getting the job done." He placed his finger on the map. "As you found out last night, this area is active." He tapped the map.

It seemed to Caden that the general was trying to decide what to say.

"The governor wants Major Westmore to know the situation he's getting in to," David said. "I think we should tell him everything."

The general looked at Fletcher.

"He's my second in command," Caden said. "I'd like him to be here."

"Okay." General Harwich took a deep breath. "The gangs cooperating with the Chinese are not reliable. While the Chinese supply them with food, drugs and guns, the members are criminals, not soldiers. They're unwilling to take orders or die for the cause."

"That isn't what we saw during the fight last night," Fletcher said.

"Do you really think you were fighting a gang?"

Caden shook his head slowly.

As sounds and smells of brewing coffee filled the room the general continued. "We believe the Chinese aided the Jihadists with planning and materials for the original terrorist attacks and we have solid intel that they are assisting them in areas of the western states not under their control. They supply the terrorists with weapons and food; even bring them in from other areas."

Caden raised an eyebrow.

"Several analysts believe China, Jihadists and perhaps Russia are dividing the country into spheres of influence. What they can't control they want balkanized. So, China assists Jihadists here, because we've resisted their efforts to control this region."

"If we knew about this, why didn't someone eliminate the terrorists weeks ago?" Fletcher asked.

"The local terrorist cell went into hiding after the blast. They've only gradually re-emerged as they secured weapons and new fighters, but we never know exactly where they are. However, it appears that last night you found them."

"How can we be sure it was them, sir?"

A broad grin grew across the general's face. "We had soldiers on scene minutes after you left. They recovered a body which we identified." Leaning back in the chair, he continued. "That is why I'm here. The Chinese are working with several groups to undermine government and law enforcement until either this region is within their sphere of influence, Balkanized or a failed state with Jihadists and gangs fighting for control. Actually, when law and order collapses the Chinese will probably move in. It's a high stakes game of international intrigue and in California and much of the southwest, they've won."

Caden rubbed his chin. "We've had MS-13 active in the Hansen area. Is that part of the Chinese effort?"

"I don't think so. Those scumbags are working their own plan."

"Oh." Caden thought of Cruz and what might be happening back home.

"We will restore law and order to all parts of western Washington as part of Operation Lexington, but first," the general inhaled deeply, "I think the coffee is ready."

Caden held the warm cup in his hands and breathed in the pleasant aroma as he returned to the table and sipped the coffee.

"We have information that the Chinese realize they will not be able to control the Pacific Northwest without a large scale military intervention and for now they are unwilling to make that effort."

"The new congress didn't support the treaty," Caden said. "Any military action would be illegal and an act of war under international law."

"Exactly. That is why they haven't moved out of the port area they now control."

Looking at Weston, Caden recalled the meeting in the parking lot where David stopped the Chinese expansion in the area and got his nose broken. "If the Chinese aren't attempting to expand their sphere of influence, that would normally be good news, but you're saying they've decided to help the terrorists."

The Colonel and Weston both nodded.

"Most of the available army units are containing the Chinese." The general made an arc around the port with his finger. "The remainder are staging here for an attack on the terrorists."

"What do you need from me?"

"We need you, and your soldiers, in combat."

*   *   *

Alone in the conference room Caden stared at the map. His orders were simple. Tomorrow they would establish a secure position for an ambush and then wait.

If all went well an army Stryker battalion would locate the Jihadists and push them toward Caden and his men. By the time the terrorists knew it was an ambush, they would be trapped in the crossfire. Death or surrender would be their only options.

He pulled the folded sheet of paper Sue had given him from his pocket and studied it. Looking at the large map on the table, he placed his index finger on the spot where his unit was ordered to deploy and used his thumb to mark Peter and Sue's home. On the map the two points were just inches away from each other.

First Sergeant Fletcher walked in and stood on the far side of the table.

Reluctantly, Caden removed his hand.

"Is that where your brother lived?"

"Yes," Caden said annoyed. "How did you know?"

"Lieutenant Brooks told me he lived in our op area and that you wanted to find out what you could."

He stood silent for a moment. Brooks was trying to be helpful, he was sure of that, but he was still irritated. Finally he sighed. "We've been busy since we got here and I don't want to endanger anyone else just because I want answers."

"If you could get Brooks to his parent's home would you do it?"

"Of course."

"I have no idea how my daughters in Florida are doing, but if you could you would help me find out."

Caden nodded.

Fletcher walked around the table. "Then sir, within our orders, there must be a way to get you to your brother's house."

An hour later they had a plan.

Caden looked over the route. "This could go wrong, so I want only volunteers with me when we head out."

*　　　　*　　　　*

The next morning as the Humvee rumbled past two mangled and burned cars, Caden pulled the map from his pocket. Progress had been slower than he had hoped through the looted and littered neighborhoods, but they would still be in position ahead of time.

"Turn left," Caden said. "Go up Hillcrest Boulevard." He grasped the radio microphone as they rolled past a looted convenience store. Not one window remained intact. "Fletcher this is Westmore. The route is still clear no contact."

"Westmore this is Fletcher. Roger."

"Do you see anything?" Caden asked the gunner, Corporal Gilbert, on top of the vehicle.

"No, sir. All quiet."

He looked over his shoulder to the young private behind him. "Do you see anything?"

"No, sir, but do you think we'll get any action?" He asked with a bit too much enthusiasm.

"Maybe later today."

The main street wound around a large modern church. Behind it was a broad parking lot and beyond that, on the right, the neighborhood was charred rubble.

Corporal Tyler looked back and forth as he drove the Humvee up the road. "The parking lot served as a fire break."

I hope Peter's house is still standing.

For the next several blocks no home survived on the right side of the road. All that remained were driveways, concrete steps, chimneys and charred wood. On the left homes were untouched by fire, but windows were broken, doors ajar. Furniture, lamps, pots and pans were scattered on the lawns. Garage doors were open, cars gone, but everything that remained was in disarray.

Gradually they drove up the slope of a large ridge. At the top, Hillcrest intersected a major thoroughfare.

The Humvee stopped.

Caden looked at Tyler.

"Sorry, it's a habit," He then proceeded across a road strewn with empty cars.

The EMP from the blast must have reached here. Caden updated his position with the convoy. "Still clear. No contact." The rest of the unit would turn west down the highway, but Caden was now on a personal mission.

The land before them was flat, but in the distance were several blackened hills.

They were close now. Reaching the far side of the main road Tyler wove around abandoned cars. Caden checked each street sign as they passed. "Turn there," he said pointing to the cul-de-sac on the right.

What will I find at Peter and Sue's home? Caden shuddered as all that he had seen this morning flashed through his mind.

Tyler maneuvered around more abandoned cars.

He pointed. "There." Caden's gut twisted in a knot at the sight of a two-story peach home. The living room window was shattered. A car sat in the driveway with one door open. Trash and debris litter the area. *What will I find inside?*

CHAPTER TWENTY THREE

The Humvee pulled up to the curb. "Stay here. Keep watch," Caden said. As he stepped onto the front porch, the smudge of a boot print was visible near the doorknob. A mild breeze brought a squeak from the door.

He placed one hand on his pistol and pushed the door open. "I'm Major Caden Westmore with the Washington Guard. If anyone is inside announce your presence."

The living room was a tempest-tossed mess of papers, bottles, pans and broken furniture. Caden couldn't recall what had been there, but he was certain there had been a couch and a TV.

He smirked. *The television might have been a nice one, but it wasn't EMP proof.*

Hearing a noise in the kitchen, he crept that way. As he looked around the corner, a rat darted across a floor strewn with flatware and broken dishes. The fridge door was open. Within were a few containers growing mold in a variety of colors.

As Caden finished checking the first floor, his radio crackled.

"Westmore, this is Transport. Golf 181 reports sporadic gunfire north of their position."

The driver of the Humvee has to tell me my men are hearing gunfire. He sighed. *I should be with them.* He turned towards the door. *Don't overreact. We've been hearing gunfire since we got here.* Standing at the bottom of the stairs, Caden said, "Transport. Roger. Do you hear anything?"

"Westmore, this is Transport. Negative. This place is as quiet as a grave."

"Transport. Roger. This shouldn't take much longer. Advise me if anything changes. Over."

Caden looked up the stairs. *Let's get this done.* He bounded up the steps two at a time, but halted as the first waves assaulted his nostrils. His gut twisted in a knot. He knew that smell—the stench of death.

From his pocket he retrieved a cloth, poured water from his canteen on it, and held it to his nose with one hand. In the other hand he held the pistol,

Caden proceeded up the stairs. *God, let it be an animal. At least not Peter.*

He opened the door to the first bedroom. The room had been used as a storeroom and the smell was weak, but he searched it anyway, looking in the closest and under a bed with no sheets. As he expected he found nothing.

In the next room, the overall hue was blue, with wallpaper showing friendly dinosaurs and sea creatures. *Sue will need the playpen and other things, but how would I get them to the farm?* When he was finished in that room he checked the bathroom off the hall, but found nothing.

"Westmore, this is Transport. The drone has sighted vehicles in the area. My guess is they heard the Humvee, like we thought they would, and now they're searching for us. No contact yet."

Caden stood at the door of the master bedroom. The smell came from inside. How many times had he seen death and smelled its grizzly scent? Reaching for the knob, he hesitated, but time was limited. *What are the chances of it being Peter? Get this done and get out of here.*

"Transport, this is Westmore. Roger. Nearly done."

Pressing the cloth to his face he opened the door.

In the shock of that moment, the smell disappeared as he processed what he saw. Lying on the right side of the bed was a man in a police uniform. Caden could not recognize the body, but as he stepped closer the nametag told him all he needed to know.

"Hello, brother." There was more that he wanted to say. If he had been part of Peter's life…If he'd been there…close enough to help…things might have…would have, turned out differently. But the thoughts and words jumbled in his mind. "I'm sorry."

Caden pressed transmit on his radio. "Send a body bag to the second floor. Then we'll be leaving."

On the nightstand was an empty pill bottle. He read the label, but learned little.

Seconds later someone ran into the house and started up the stairs. Progress slowed after a few steps. When the young private arrived at the bedroom door he dropped the bag and puked repeatedly in the hall.

The sound of engines and squealing tires caught his attention. *Probably not good news.* "Come on private. Open up the bag on the other side of the bed. We're going to use the bedspread to lift him and set in it."

The private, pale as the sheets, nodded.

The radio crackled. "Westmore this is Transport. Vehicles approaching. They've found us. Advise you return at once."

Caden pulled the bedspread and flipped it over his brother.

The private moved the hand from his face and gagged. "He's holding something."

The lower part of his brother's right hand stuck out from under the cover. In that hand was a plastic bag with folded paper in it.

Gunfire erupted.

Caden grabbed the plastic bag and put it in a pocket.

The private winced as shots hit the house and ricocheted.

The Humvee 50 caliber returned fire.

"I'll take the bedspread at the head, you take it at the feet and we'll slide him off the bed into the bag."

The private nodded, winced, retched and grabbed the cover in one continuous motion.

"Westmore, this is Transport. Now would be a good time to go."

Caden didn't answer. He zipped the bag and pointed to the far end. "Grab it. Let's move!"

As they came down the stairs, Caden spoke into his radio. "Transport this is Westmore. We're coming out. Provide cover."

The 50 cal fired continuously.

The private held the bag in one hand and opened the front door of the house with his free one.

The Humvee had moved closer to the house, blocking most angles of fire.

As the private stepped on the porch, he stumbled.

"Are you hit?" Caden shouted over the roar of fire.

Without answering, he regained his footing and raced to the vehicle, opened the door and jumped in pulling the body bag with him.

Caden followed into the front passenger side. "Go! Go! Go!"

The engine roared.

As the Humvee bounced onto the road, Caden scanned the route. Three vehicles blocked the end of the cul-de-sac. The black flag of jihad flew from one SUV.

From atop the Humvee, Gilbert fired steadily as six or more terrorists shot back from behind the cars. Shell casings jingled as they fell on and in the vehicle.

Two terrorists moved into flanking positions and fired.

Bullets pinged off the Humvee.

Caden spotted a man aiming a rocket propelled grenade. "Left! Swerve left!"

The Humvee bounded up the curb and onto a lawn.

"Fire right," Caden shouted.

The sound of gunfire, ricochets and brass was deafening.

Gilbert turned and unleashed a steady barrage at the terrorist with the RPG. Then he cursed and fell into the main compartment and onto Peter's body.

Caden looked over his shoulder.

"Brace!" Tyler yelled.

The Humvee hit one car spinning it out of the way.

Caden slammed into his seatbelt.

An agonized scream came from outside.

As the Humvee continued to accelerate down the road, Caden turned to check on Gilbert.

Amazingly the corporal was moving Peter's body into the back, out of the way.

"Are you okay?" Caden asked.

Gilbert put two fingers in bullet holes near his heart. "Thank God for Kevlar."

"You're going to have one heck of a bruise." Caden sighed. "Have the medic check you when we rendezvous with Golf 181."

Still smiling, Gilbert nodded.

Only then did Caden notice the young private was bleeding.

Turning to Gilbert, he said, "Corporal, I need you up there providing cover fire."

The soldier gave a reluctant nod and climbed back into position.

The private was ghostly pale. Blood stained much of his torso and hip. "Where were you hit?"

"They're following," Gilbert yelled and fired.

Gently the private touched a spot high on his side.

Again, came the ping of ricochets and brass tingling as it fell from the gun.

"Is that the only place you're hurt?"

He nodded. "I think so."

Clumsily, Caden crawled into the back and finished moving his brother's body out of the way. "I need to see the wound."

The young man gritted his teeth and moaned, as Caden helped remove his bloody jacket. He thought he knew everyone in the unit, but not this young man. Glancing at his nametag he said, "What's your first name, Private Conner?"

"Steve…Steven, sir."

Finding a tear in the bloody shirt, Caden ripped it wider.

The young man winced.

"How long have you been with the unit?"

"I joined three weeks ago. I'm the newest guy they sent on the operation."

After wiping some of the blood away, with gauze from the first aid kit, Caden got a good look at the wound. "Where are you from, Steve?"

"Hansen. I graduated from the high school last June."

Caden showed the young man the wound in his side. It was a jagged cut, but only skin deep. "It almost missed you." He wrapped and bandaged Conner's chest. "Yesterday you were a boy from Hansen, a raw recruit. Today you're a combat veteran." He smiled. "Welcome to the club."

Conner smiled as Caden finished applying the bandages.

"Keep pressure on the wound with your hand. The medics will look at it when we rejoin the unit in a minute or two." Caden crawled back into the front seat and called over the radio. "Golf 181, this is Westmore. We are in route to your location, being pursued and under fire. Over."

Fletcher's voice came over the radio. "Roger. The welcome wagons will be ready."

Looking straight ahead Tyler shouted, "We got problems."

Caden had already seen it. Up ahead, three cars moved into position to block the road. "Go left through the strip mall."

As they bounced through the parking lot, Caden reported the situation to Fletcher.

The Humvee bounced over a speed bump.

The private moaned.

Gilbert slammed to his left. "Hey Tyler, maybe I could aim if you didn't hit everything."

"Hold on," Tyler yelled and drove the Humvee off the curb and back onto the road.

Gilbert cursed and fired.

Over the radio came Fletcher's calm voice. "Bravo 200 is approaching from the north where a drone has located a suspicious group."

"Roger. If that group is not the target have them close on our position ASAP because I definitely have Jihadists on my tail."

Gilbert collapsed into the back seat. Blood soaked his uniform.

"See what you can do for him," Caden said to Conner and crawled toward the gun hatch.

Thunder reverberated through the Humvee.

The vehicle lurched left, then right, then flipped upside down.

CHAPTER TWENTY FOUR

Out of the foggy darkness, Caden heard Fletcher's voice. "We gotta go. Can you move?"

Gradually his eyes focused. There was a seat above him. Caden shook his head. The Humvee was upside down.

Fletcher, on his hands and knees, was half in and out where a window should have been.

Bullets pinged off the Humvee.

At the sound of cursing, Caden looked forward. Tyler hung upside and, using a knife, cut the seat belt.

Gilbert was sprawled nearby. A gaping wound to his head told Caden he was dead.

"Where's Conner?"

"Outside providing cover." Fletcher backed out of the Humvee. "Let's get out of here."

Tyler plopped down with more cursing.

Caden grabbed an M4 and crawled out. Bullets pinged and ricocheted around him.

Corporal Tyler followed, slapped a magazine into his rifle and, when a ricochet whipped by, said, "It was safer hanging upside down in the Humvee!"

"How many shooters?" Caden asked.

Fletcher fired. "Six maybe seven."

The muzzle flash smacked Caden across his face. He turned and saw a man fall.

Conner fired from behind a nearby concrete barrier as terrorists attacked from his right.

After pulling his pistol from the holster, Caden fired at two others. "We need to get out of here. Where are the rest of the soldiers?"

"The army made contact..." Fletcher fired a three round burst. "...with the terrorists, but they hightailed it south, just like we expected."

Both men fired.

Another terrorist fell.

"I took a few men to look for you when you didn't show." Fletcher shot to his right. "Figured you were close. Most of the soldiers are at the southern chokepoint of the trap."

Bullets slammed into the Humvee.

Caden pointed to a six foot cement planter nearby and shouted to Tyler. "Can you get there if we provide cover?"

He nodded.

"Go!" Caden said.

Both he and Fletcher fired continuous bursts.

Tyler slid behind it like a runner going into home plate, gave a thumb's up to Caden, and began shooting.

"Where are the men with you?" Caden asked.

Fletcher point in one direction and then fired in another.

Caden changed magazines, shot a terrorist, and then looked where Fletcher had pointed. Three soldiers fired from the roof of a nearby drugstore. Others shot from windows. "That's a better position."

Bullets slammed the ground inches from them throwing asphalt and dust in their faces.

"You don't need to tell me that," Fletcher said.

Over the roar of battle Conner yelled, "RPG!"

Caden turned, saw the man with the launcher and shot, but missed. He smacked Fletcher on the shoulder. "Run!"

Fletcher raced toward the drugstore.

Caden and Tyler provided cover.

A shooter slammed back against a car and collapsed.

Conner stood behind the concrete barrier, and fired repeated bursts.

The Jihadist with the RPG fell.

Two terrorists shot at Conner.

The private fell back hitting the ground with a thud.

Tyler returned fire hitting one of the shooters.

Caden shot at the other.

Silence reigned over the area.

"Cover me." Caden shouted. He ran to Conner and pulled him to a safer spot. The only sound Caden heard was his heart pounding in his ears. He knelt and pressed two fingers to the young soldier's neck but couldn't find a pulse. "First Sergeant, have the men check the enemy positions."

"You heard him. Secure the area, check the bodies." Fletcher shouted. "But be careful. Some of them could be alive." Fletcher then jogged over to Caden. "How is Conner?"

In the distance came the sound of gunfire.

"Dead." Caden closed the young soldier's eyes.

The radio on both Caden and Fletcher crackled. "Fletcher, this is Golf 181. "Engaging the enemy."

"Golf 181, this is Westmore. We will be approaching from the rear."

"Roger that. Glad to hear your voice."

Caden turned to Fletcher. "Do we have a vehicle?"

"No, but we're less than a mile from the chokepoint."

"Okay, we run back," Caden said. "Let's do a quick intel check while the men collect gear and rig a stretcher for Conner's body." He looked back at the overturned Humvee. "I need to get something."

Minutes later, as Caden slid the body of his brother from the vehicle; he heard the crunch of gravel and looked up.

"We have eight dead Jihadists," Fletcher said. "We have two walking wounded. Our only causalities were Private Conner and Gilbert, but…who…ah, is this your brother?"

"Yes." Caden stared at the bag. He thought he should feel something, but he didn't. He wiped the sweat from his brow. "Are we ready to move out, First Sergeant?"

"Yes, sir, but before we go sir, remember you told me to pick from the volunteers for your part of this operation?"

Caden nodded.

"Well, every man in the unit volunteered."

"Everyone?"

"Yes, sir. I added Conner because I figured he would be safer with you."

"I guess I would have thought the same. Thanks, First Sergeant.

Caden scanned the area and shouted. "Okay, we've got more fighting to do so, let's move out." Along with another man, Caden hoisted Peter's body and ran toward the next fight.

*   *   *

Caden handed the mic back to the radio operator after providing his preliminary post-battle report. The terrorists had hit them hard. Seven were dead, fifteen wounded. Four were serious; a chopper from the logistics base was inbound for them. The rest were well enough to return with the unit.

As he walked away he felt strangely detached, like a ghost haunting the living. He saw, but only vaguely perceived.

He moved without direction.

The air was still.

No dogs barked.

No birds chirped.

This had been a park beside a river. The grass was green, but not mowed. To his left was a towering bridge. The sun shone on all of it.

He felt nothing.

Only then did he realize he stood among the dead.

Eight body bags lay in a line before him.

He knelt by the first body bag. Slowly he unzipped it, looked the soldier in the face. "Corporal Gilbert. You were the best marksman in your squad."

He moved on to the next. "Private Chambers. You were brave and always the first to volunteer."

The dead eyes of the next soldier stared up at Caden and twisted his gut into a knot. "Private Steven Conner. I learned your name just an hour ago. Thank you for having my back." *So many have died.* He looked down the row of dead and remembered one of them was his brother. Thoughts of Peter stirred emotion back into him. In a voice barely above a whisper he asked, "Why God?"

"They say that God puts us where we need to be."

Caden stood and looked at Fletcher. "I shouldn't have said that out loud. It's not good for soldiers to ask existential questions."

"I'm not sure what existential means, but I think we all ask God why things happen." Looking at Conner the first sergeant said, "I think he saved you."

Caden followed his gaze. "He provided cover fire that gave you time to get to me and stayed on point. He may have saved us both."

"True," Fletcher said. "However, in the big scheme of things I don't matter, but you do."

Caden cast him a questioning look. "You matter to me and to a lot of the soldiers."

"Yes, sir, I'm not saying people don't care for each other, it's…well…Hansen wouldn't have survived without Sheriff Hoover, but he was just trying to save the town."

"What about Brooks? What about you?"

"Me? I'm no leader, just a good follower. Brooks, he'll be a fine officer in a few years, but when you came he was just trying to keep things together at the armory. You were the one that got people working on the power plant, you had the idea of finding greenhouses and you stopped Durant's forces at the causeway. You had vision."

Caden felt his face flush at Fletcher's tribute, as he recalled the verse in Proverbs, 'Where there is no vision, the people perish.' He remembered the preacher asking, 'Who will stand in the gap,' and the Chaplain talking about rebuilding what had been broken. He looked at the row of fallen soldiers. "Perhaps we are all exactly where God needs us, but I'm sorry they needed to be here."

Fletcher nodded.

Soldier's arrived and carried off the bodies.

Caden and Fletcher headed back toward the vehicles.

Thinking of Maria, Caden said, "I wonder how everyone is doing back in Hansen."

"We left on Monday and it's what…Thursday? How much could go wrong?"

CHAPTER TWENTY FIVE

Maria yawned as she turned into the hospital parking lot. It was just after eight in the morning, and she had been up since dropping Caden off at the armory. *This is going to be a long Monday. I'll take a nap in the waiting room while Sue sees the doctor.*

She had planned to let Sue off at the hospital entrance and then park the car, but a Humvee blocked the lane. A soldier stood outside signaling them to pull into the parking lot.

"I'll get us as close as I can," she said with a frown.

"I can walk," Sue said. "I'm just slow and I waddle."

Both women laughed.

Maria pulled into a spot across from the main doors. A police car, with lights flashing, was right where she would have dropped Sue off. *What's going on?* She helped Sue out of the car.

As they walked toward the building, Sue gestured with her eyes toward the homeless people camped along the edge of the lot. "They always make me nervous, but today I think we have plenty of protection."

Maria smiled anxiously. "Yes, but why are they all here?"

"Who cares? I'm just thankful they are."

Though it was still early, about a dozen people were in the lobby. A nurse sat behind a long counter. A janitor mopped in the corner. The rest were waiting patients.

"Oh, look, down the hall, isn't that David with the deputy? And the guy between them, is he the one you were talking about?"

Maria looked to her right and immediately recognized both Brooks and Cruz.

"He has a lot of tattoos."

Maria shuddered. "Let's go the other way, okay?" She turned,

155

and holding Sue's arm, led her toward a door on their left.

As they approached the lobby exit a shot rang out.

Maria spun around.

The janitor held a gun still pointed at the falling deputy.

The room erupted in chaos and screams.

Brooks spun toward the shooter, dropping to his knee as he did, and fired.

The janitor collapsed to the floor.

Cruz, still in hand and leg cuffs, raced out the door.

Steady gunfire raged outside the building.

Beside Maria, a man stood slowly and aimed at Brooks.

"David!" She hit the man with her fist.

The gunman turned and, with an amused expression, pointed his weapon at Maria.

What can I do? Maria forced her eyes from the gun to the man.

Three quick shots threw the man over the row of seats.

David's eyes scanned the room as he slowly stood. He motioned for Maria to come and then handed her the deputy's pistol. "Where's Sue?"

"She was with me a minute ago."

"Find her and stay safe. I've got to go." Crouching he ran outside.

With the gun at the ready, Maria trotted across the lobby.

A woman, hiding behind chairs, muffled a scream.

"I'm one of the good guys...gals, whatever," Maria said. "Sue where are you?" Continuing in the direction they had gone, Maria pushed one side of the nearby double doors, but it opened only partway before it bumped against something. Hearing rapid breathing, she stepped through on the other side.

With only her head and shoulders off the floor, Sue lay against the wall. She braced her large belly with both hands as panicked breaths ushered in and out.

"Are you okay?"

She nodded. "I think today...just became...the day."

Through the window in the door Maria saw two security guards rush across the lobby. Not wanting to get shot by a nervous security guard, she placed the gun in her jacket pocket. "I'll get a wheelchair."

"No." Sue gritted her teeth and moaned. "Don't leave. Help me stand." When Sue was on her feet she asked, "Is David okay?"

Maria looked over her shoulder into the room she had just left. "I don't know. I'll get you situated and then I'll check." Still looking through the window in the door her eyes focused on the fallen deputy and then the two gunmen. She wanted to cry, to scream, but nothing came.

Sue leaned on Maria and together they walked slowly toward the maternity unit.

*   *   *

Zach adjusted the scope on his AR-15. After he helped load the convoy, he returned home, packed camping gear and established a primitive campsite on the rock outcrop across from Bo's house. Over the last two days the crook had left the house about nine in the morning, but today he caught Zach by surprise when he departed before dawn.

You've got to come home sometime Bo. Using a bipod, Zach had his rifle aimed at the front door.

As he watched the house, the sun had risen to an orange splotch on the horizon and now it was a yellow disk peeking over the trees. The breeze coming off the coast was cool, but he could no longer see his breath. Birds chirped, somewhere a dog barked, and children laughed, but there was no Bo.

Watching the house, Zach's hatred for Bo boiled within him like a witch's brew. *Somebody should kill him. Why not me? I have every right to. Get back here Bo so I can finish this!*

He was so consumed by his own thoughts that he didn't hear Bo's Cadillac approach. Leisurely, the car pulled into the driveway and stopped. The bodyguard exited and then Bo.

Why were you out so early, Bo? As he watched the man through the scope, Zach tried to control his breathing. His heart pounded in his chest and thumped in his ears.

Zach sucked in a deep breath and placed his finger on the trigger. *Why not kill him now?* Bo spoke a few words to the driver and then walked casually toward the house. *He supplied mom with booze and drugs. She's in a coma because of him. He nearly killed her. Pull the trigger! Kill him!*

But he didn't.

Bo stepped into the house.

He cursed and closed his eyes. *Zach, you're a coward, a worthless coward!*

Bo stumbled backward out of the house and almost fell to the ground.

Four Hispanic men poured out.

Zach pressed his eye to the scope. *MS-13? It looks like the same guys. Is that Cruz? How did he get out?*

The bodyguard pulled his gun.

Two of the gang members shot him.

Zach gasped.

Bo screamed like a girl.

Cruz pushed Bo toward the Cadillac. "Come on, let's take a ride."

Zach was surprised how much he could hear in the stillness of early morning.

Stepping on the bodyguard's arm, one of the other men pulled the gun from the fallen man's hand, stuffed it in his pocket and walked on.

Behind Bo was his car. Around him the gang members formed an ever tightening semi-circle.

"I haven't been able to find him. He hasn't been at his house for days!" Bo nearly screamed.

That's because I've been spending most of my time watching you.

"What about his mommy and daddy?" Cruz asked.

Bo's head twitched from person to person. "His dad is dead. Mom is in a coma."

Gee, did we miss each other at the hospital?

"That's too bad," Cruz said. "You haven't been very useful, and now I don't see that you would be any help."

"Sister. He has a sister."

"See, now wasn't that easy. She knows where he is. Let's go find her."

Quickly they pushed Bo into the car and sped away.

Vicki! Zach gulped, and then jumped to his feet with the realization that his sister was at the hospital. *No, it's DeLynn at the house. What will they do when they find her?*

Slinging the rifle on his back, Zach ran into the forest. With

158

panic-induced speed he sprinted in the direction of his home as he tried to come up with a plan. *The car will have to take the road around Palmer Ridge.* Images of trails and topography flashed through his mind. The first part of the path went uphill, but the last portion was mostly down. It would be tough, but he might be able to arrive before the car.

He knew DeLynn had a cell phone, now he wished he did.

He ran.

He prayed.

God, I know I wanted to kill Bo, but please don't let DeLynn be hurt just because I'm no good. Please keep Vicki at the hospital. Please keep DeLynn safe.

Branches smacked his face and arms as he ran with fear-inspired haste along the trail. Within minutes sweat rolled down his forehead. His heart rate climbed as his feet raced up the hill. Breathing came in quick rasps.

Where he could, he left the path and scampered up the hill instead of following the gradual incline and switchbacks of the trail.

He stumbled, tore his jeans and felt the warm dampness of blood, but any first-aid would have to wait.

Reaching the ridgeline he bent over to catch his breath. When he could, he wiped the sweat from his brow, stood erect, and unzipped his coat. Still taking in great drafts of air, he searched the highway hundreds of feet below for any sign of Bo's car. There was none.

Many times he had stood in this spot taking in the vista of the valley below, but not this time. After a quick look at the cut on his leg, and a deep breath, he took off on the downhill portion of his run.

By the time he reached the road he was breathing heavily. Using the tree line for cover he ran along the road. Nearing a short bridge over a creek, he stepped from the trees. Normally, several cars would be traveling along here during the day. Zach looked up and down the empty road. *Who could find or afford gas?* Then he answered his own question. *Bo could, but where is his car now?*

He spat, took a deep breath and ran on toward his home.

The other side of this hill is my house, but if I stay on the road I risk being seen. With a sigh he ran up the last hill.

As he neared the rusty blue trailer he heard a car pull up. Aware of his heavy breathing, he dared not approach any closer until he could be silent.

When his breathing was normal, Zach inched toward his home. Staying low he used the brush as cover. He caught glimpses of Cruz, Bo and the others, but couldn't understand what was being said. He edged slowly closer, just as he had done many times when hunting a deer or elk. When he was behind a moss and fern covered stump, he saw Cruz holding a gun to Bo's back as the two stood in the driveway. Another gang member leaned against the car.

Zach was sure he was close enough to hear, but no one was saying anything. Carefully he removed the rifle from his back and, using the scope, turned to the trailer as a commotion came from inside.

Two thugs dragged a tearful DeLynn from the house and forced her to her knees about ten feet from Bo.

Zach's heart pounded in his ears. His finger touched the trigger.

DeLynn leaned forward into Zach's line of fire.

His finger jumped off the trigger.

"Now that we've got the sister, we don't need you," Cruz said.

Bo looked at DeLynn, but remained silent.

In the middle of the driveway, Cruz forced Bo to his knees and shot him in the head.

CHAPTER TWENTY SIX

DeLynn screamed.

Zach stifled a gasp as he looked through the scope for a target, but the gang scurried for the car. One of them grabbed DeLynn by the hair and threw her in the backseat. Cruz and the driver were already in. Before he could decide what to do, the Cadillac roared down the driveway.

Zach watched as it turned left onto the main road and disappeared. *DeLynn!* His stomach twisted into knots.

Remembering Bo, he sprinted to where he lay and pressed two fingers to his neck. The bloody wound was severe enough that he wasn't surprised when he detected no pulse. *What am I going to do? Call the police? No, I need to follow them—but how?*

A young neighbor boy stood at the edge of the woods staring at Zach with his mouth agape.

"It's not what you think. I didn't shoot him."

The wide-eyed kid darted into the woods.

Suddenly, he had a plan. Zach raced down the driveway and across the road to the Hollister home. He was about to bang wildly on the front door, but instead paused, drew a deep breath and knocked politely. Zach cradled his rifle and waited.

As he expected, the door cracked open but, when DeLynn's father saw Zach and tried to shut it, he kicked it hard.

"DeLynn is in trouble." He said stepping into the house. "I don't have time to explain. Where are your car keys?"

"What kind of trouble? You're stealing my car?"

"Borrowing. Get me the keys now!" He brandished the gun in the man's direction.

"Okay. Okay. Has DeLynn been hurt?" Mr. Hollister slid the

keys across a table.

Zach grabbed them. "Call the sheriff and tell them to go to my house. Do it now!" He ran for the garage.

Watching the garage door go up was slow motion agony. Zach squealed the tires backing out and ran off the driveway into the yard before arching back onto the road. Then he pursued the Cadillac, prayed he would find it, and wondered what to do when he did.

*   *   *

Hoover walked toward the body in the driveway. It hadn't surprised him when Caden said Bo and Zach knew each other. Zach had been on his radar for years and if there was an illegal sale of alcohol, tobacco or pot in the county, Bo was probably involved. The two were bound to come together.

The sheriff stared at the body, face down in the dirt of the driveway. *If anyone was going to supply Zach's drunk of a mother with booze or drugs, it would be you. But you were always good at keeping your hands clean. I never had quite enough to arrest you.*

The sheriff looked over his shoulder as a detective exited the trailer. "What have you found?"

"We have witnesses that saw Zach argue with the victim at the Library Park market a few days ago. A kid saw Zach standing over the body moments after hearing the gunshot. Zach is still missing, along with the Hollister girl and their car. The young man clearly had means, motive and the opportunity to kill Bo. My initial conclusion is the victim came here. They quarreled. Zach killed him, and fled with DeLynn Hollister."

Hoover stared at the body. "Sounds reasonable, but did DeLynn go willingly, or was she kidnapped?"

The detective shrugged. "The boy's comments to Kent Hollister make that unclear, but when we find the boy, I'm certain we'll find the girl.

What did all that cleverness get you, Bo? As the EMTs lifted him onto the gurney, Hoover looked over the body. *A single bullet to the head—execution style. The kid has a mean streak.* "Why do you think Zach told Mr. Hollister to call 9-1-1?"

The deputy shrugged.

"The boy has a sister, right?"

"Yeah, Vicki. She was at the hospital all night with the mother."

Hoover stifled his amusement that it was a boy that finally got Bo. From what Caden had told him, he could hardly blame the kid. Hoover thought of his own mother barely hanging on to life in the hospital. *If someone treated her like Bo treated Zach's mom....* He sighed. "Issue an arrest warrant for Zach Brennon and advise that he is armed and dangerous."

*   *   *

When Zach spotted the Cadillac it wasn't difficult to follow. They weren't speeding, but it was tough to remain inconspicuous in a red sedan with no other cars on the road. They had such a lead that he nearly missed when they turned onto the gravel logging road. *Why are they going into the national forest?*

Zach parked the car. *Think! Think! Why would an urban gang take this road? Where are they going?* He had walked this road several times while hunting. Now he tried to imagine it in his mind. Any good map showed the road connecting with two others, that exited in the next county, but those crossed over high ridgelines and were still snowbound. He laughed at the thought of urban gangsters stuck in snow on a primitive logging road. Only the thought of DeLynn, stranded in the cold with a bunch of killers, chilled his amusement.

Assuming they don't want to go to the next county, why would they turn up this road? In his mind he walked up the road. Almost immediately he recalled the ranger station. Normally, the modern wood frame building would be staffed by a couple of rangers, but with the bad economy, faltering paper money, and failing government, the rangers probably hadn't been paid and were forced to fend for themselves and their families. He hoped he was right, and they weren't there. Cruz and the others would kill anyone they stumbled across.

Zach looked in the direction they had gone. *How did they find this hideout?* Sure, logging roads were in most GPS systems and the station was even marked on many maps. Still it was a stretch to imagine that they had been driving around and found it. Perhaps Bo knew about it, but that seemed unlikely. Driving logging roads was not his style. No matter how they found the cabin, it would be a good hiding place. About a mile off the main road and, he hoped, deserted.

He put the car in drive and headed up the gravel road to a wide spot. There he parked it behind brush and bramble to hide it. Stepping from the car, he looked up the road. *I'm sure getting my exercise today.* He sprinted into the forest and followed the road toward his destination.

The station sat in small clearing about a mile off the paved road. Sunlight poured down on the simple brown building that served as the headquarters for rangers in the area. Normally, he would go in and talk with the rangers, but not today. In front of the building, the road widened allowing cars to pull off and park. There was only one vehicle there, Bo's Cadillac.

Okay, I'm here, now how am I going to rescue DeLynn. He thought DeLynn would be safe until they had secured his cooperation. At least, he hoped that would be true—prayed it would be true.

It's simple really, I either kill them all before they can hurt DeLynn or convince them to stay and not hurt her until I can get help. He sighed. *God help me. I know this is all my fault, but…well, help DeLynn, if you can't help me. I wish Major Westmore was in town.*

He sat thinking for several minutes until he determined there was only one way. He hid the rifle in a Vine Maple at the edge of the forest. Then he positioned himself behind a nearby tree and shouted. "Cruz, this is Zach. I hear you're looking for me. Let's talk."

For several moments nothing happened. Zach was about to try again when he saw the door creak open.

Then DeLynn stumbled into the doorway.

Zach could see an arm reaching across to the back of his girlfriend's head. *I could grab the rifle, shoot through the wall, and kill whoever is holding her.* He shook his head. *No, the others would kill her.*

Cruz called from the cabin. "Yeah, let's talk kid. No guns or your sister dies."

Sister? They think she's my sister. He wasn't sure whether that was good or bad, but for the moment he decided the less they knew, the better. "And I want to talk to my sister."

"Sure. You first kid. And I want to see your hands."

Zach sucked in a deep breath. As he slowly let it out he stepped from behind the tree into the light, but with Bo's car between him and the cabin.

With a push on the back of the head, DeLynn lurched

forward and Cruz followed. The thug held his girlfriend by her hair.

DeLynn's face was pale and her cheeks streaked with tears.

"Have they hurt you?" Zach asked.

She shook her head.

"I want to see all of you. Move out from behind the car."

Zach moved slowly and kept the car between him and much of the cabin."

"My friends in the house could kill you and we could keep this pretty thing as a prize, but I'd rather do business with you. Bo seemed to think you can get M4s, magazines and ammo for me."

Zach nodded. He had no idea how he could steal them, but he knew his only option was to agree. "It will be difficult and the soldiers...."

"That's your problem. I need as many as you can get. Twenty is a nice number. I can give you three...."

"Five days. I'll need five and let her go while I...."

Cruz laughed. "Four days. That way we will leave while the good people of this community are still asleep or in church—and the girl stays with us."

"When I steal the guns the soldiers that do the inventory will notice. It won't take them long to figure it out and come hunting for me."

"Again, amigo, that is your problem. After we settle a couple of scores, we will be moving on to another town. Maybe you'll be moving on, too." Cruz rubbed his chin. "About the scores we need to settle, do you know anyone who is good with a bow?"

DeLynn's eyes grew wide and her face paler.

Zach shook his head. "I can't help you with that."

"Okay." Cruz smiled, released DeLynn's hair and put his arm around her. "I don't want to hurt her. Family is important, but this is business."

Zach locked eyes with DeLynn. "She is family and I do love her. Keep her safe and I'll be back on Sunday."

Placing his hand over his heart Cruz said, "Really touching, kid. You bring me twenty M4s and I guarantee you two go home safe. You bring me nineteen...." Cruz put his hand to DeLynn's head like a gun. "Pow."

"I understand."

"A couple of things I should mention. It's not smart to follow us on a deserted road in a red car. Since you know about this place, we'll be leaving. Don't try to follow us again or we kill you both."

Cruz shoved DeLynn forward, pulled a phone from his pocket and slid it along the trunk of the car. When you get the guns call the number in that phone. You can be early, but don't be late and don't bring the law, or she'll be the first one to die." Cruz smiled. "Do the right thing."

Zach nodded. *If she dies, you die with her.* "There won't be any police."

"Good. Then I'll see you no later than…let's say nine on Sunday."

How late do you think we sleep in around here? A lot of people will be up by then.

Cruz grabbed DeLynn's hair and backed toward the cabin.

He was reluctant to turn away from his girlfriend, but it was best to be in the cover of the woods before Cruz had a chance to change his mind. Zach retrieved his rifle and raced for the car.

I've got to find Lieutenant Brooks and somehow contact Major Westmore and First Sergeant Fletcher. They'll know what to do. I should have just gone back to the armory when they went up the logging road. The car disappeared around a curve. *I'm so stupid.*

As he backed the Hollister car onto the road, he still hadn't seen Bo's car. *They're taking their time leaving the ranger station.*

Twenty minutes later Zach was relieved to see the armory. He rolled down the window as he drove up to the sentry.

"Nice car, Zach. Is it yours?" The sentry asked.

"Where's Lieutenant Brooks? I need to talk to him."

"You didn't hear? He was shot Monday morning and is still in intensive care."

"Who's in charge?"

"Sergeant Adams, I think."

Zach shook his head. The sergeant was just a few years older than him. There was no way he would authorize the kind of operation Zach needed.

He pulled into the parking lot and thought for several minutes. *I have two choices, somehow steal the weapons, or go convince Hoover to help me. Two lousy options.* His stomach was a churning vat of worry. *With all the soldiers gone I don't think there are twenty rifles in the vault for me to steal. One lousy option.* Zach turned the car around and headed for the sheriff's office.

What else can I do to rescue DeLynn? He racked his brain for another plan, but every time it came down to steal the guns or get help. *I'm not going to give them guns. They'll kill me and DeLynn—just like they did Bo.*

By the time he bottomed out the car on a speed bump coming into the sheriff's office parking lot, he was convinced this was his only option. Parking across two spaces he flung the rifle on his back and ran into the building. "I've got to see Sheriff Hoover."

The startled deputy just inside pulled his gun and shouted, "Drop the rifle! Get down on the ground!"

Inching his hands up, Zach shook his head. "No, you don't understand."

With his free hand the deputy fingered something under the counter.

A moment later another deputy raced from the office, followed by Hoover. Both had guns pointed at him.

"Down on the ground. Spread your arms—now," the sheriff commanded.

Zach fell to his knees and then forward onto the ground.

The sheriff kept his pistol pointed while the other two removed the rifle, handcuffed Zach and dragged him to his feet.

The sheriff nonchalantly holstered his gun, then the two locked eyes. "Zach Brennon, you are under arrest for the murder of Robert Bo Hendricks."

CHAPTER TWENTY SEVEN

The sun hung low in the sky as Caden's Humvee approached the base after the battle with the terrorists.

"Well, look at that," Corporal Tyler said.

On the corner facing them was a large wooden sign painted with wavy stripes of red, white and blue, along with the words, "Camp Victory."

When the Humvee turned the corner, Caden saw a huge American flag flying on the roof of the five-story building.

The battle, the huge flag and the time of day all brought to Caden's mind the words of the anthem, "What so proudly we hailed at the twilight's last gleaming." He smiled and said, "It's good to see that the banner yet waves."

"Over the land of the free and the home of the brave," Tyler added.

The corporal stopped in front of the main building. Caden jumped out and hurried inside. General Harwich was waiting.

After salutes, Caden said, "With your permission General, I'd like to check on my wounded men that were brought in earlier and brief you later?"

"Three of them were treated and sent on to the army hospital. They're doing okay. The fourth man didn't make it." The general set his hand on Caden's shoulder. "I'm sorry. Get some rest. We'll talk tomorrow at 0900."

Alone in the room that was both his office and sleeping quarters, Caden sighed deeply, walked to the desk and sat with a thud. As he did, he heard a crinkling sound and, from his pocket, retrieved a plastic bag.

He hadn't forgotten about what he pulled from Peter's dead

hand. He couldn't forget such a thing. It had just been a busy day.

Childhood memories of Peter and family flitted through his mind. He didn't know how long he stared into the air thinking of the brother he would never again see, but when he became aware of his surroundings, the sun barely peeked over the horizon.

He turned on the desk lamp and opened the bag. Inside, a sheet of paper was folded around an envelope. On the paper was a handwritten note. Caden took a slow, deep breath and read.

To whoever finds this;

My name is Peter Westmore. I am a sergeant with the Renton Police Department assisting the Seattle P.D. with the evacuation before the blast. We didn't know where or when the bomb would go off, but when it did I knew immediately that I was too close. The roads were clogged before the blast. The growing mushroom cloud, storm of dust and snow-like fallout only made it worse.

The doctor at the medical station told me what I already know; the dose of radiation I received is lethal. They wanted to keep me at the medical facility, but I didn't want to die there. I needed to find my wife and make sure she is safe.

By the time I reached the house it was deserted and I am too weak to go on. Please, whoever finds this, get the enclosed letter to my family in Hansen. The address is on the envelope.

Peter Westmore

Caden unfolded the envelope. It was addressed to Sue. He stared at it and hoped there were words of comfort in it for her and perhaps a message for the rest of the family. Carefully he refolded the letter and returned it to the bag.

He wiped his eyes. How many loved ones had he lost this year? How many tears had he shed? How much pain was there left to endure?

The terrorists killed my brother, killed Private Conner, and six...no seven, others today. They killed Maria's entire family, Adam's mother and millions of others I never knew.

He thought of his men, wounded during the fight earlier in the day, and the scars they would carry. *Millions of others were burned in the blast, scared by violence or traumatized.* He thought of the two girls that ran to the base. *Amy and Beth will carry the pain of their ordeal to the grave.*

Terrorists, Jihadists, Islamists, Communists in China and North

Korea, or gang members it didn't matter what they called themselves, it was evil, soul-rotting evil. He struggled to understand how it happened that evil men from around the globe had united to destroy the nation he loved. *How could evil be so logical, so strategic?*

He had no answers.

The sun succumbed to the night, leaving only the feeble glow of his desk lamp to push back the gloom. Darkness ruled his world and, like a contagion, infected him.

He recalled the dead suicidal terrorists who set off the Seattle bomb and the others who died earlier that day.

I hate them—all of them. I'm glad I killed a few today.

*   *   *

As a bugler sounded reveille, Caden rolled to a sitting position in his bunk and wondered when he went to bed. He had no duties until the briefing with the general and so, after a minute, plopped back on his pillow.

When he next opened his eyes, the morning sun poured through the window. He checked his watch. It was still early. Dressed in socks and underwear, he moved his desk chair near the window, sat, and let the sun's warmth sink deeply into him.

For nearly a half hour he remained there, writing a citation for bravery for Private Conner, and a letter to Maria.

As he washed and dressed, he recalled the anger of the night before. There was still a great sadness in him for the friends and loved ones who had died, but a good night's sleep and a warm sun had driven the foul mood from him. Instead of hate he was filled with resolve. His mother would say, 'hate the sin, but love the sinner.' He couldn't bring himself to love the terrorists but, in the light of day, he knew it was evil that he hated—and he would work to ensure that brooding malevolence didn't hurt anyone else he cared for.

It was still early, so Caden decided to take in the sun and view from the roof. Walking along the parapet, he noticed a line of people coming through a makeshift gate in a sandbag wall. Some of the civilians carried suitcases. One man pushed a wheelbarrow with kids and clothes in it. Others had nothing but the clothes they wore.

Caden turned to a nearby soldier. "What's going on over there?"

"They're refugees coming in from the city."

"I didn't realize that many people still remained in the area."

"You weren't here yesterday, were you, sir?"

Caden shook his head. "I had business off base."

"Well sir, a unit from here and another from the JBLM fought some of the remaining terrorists. You could hear the shooting from where we're standing."

"You could?"

"Yes, sir. And I guess a lot of people decided that was the time to leave because several hundred came in during the battle."

"I wish I could have been here to see that." Caden said with a facetious grin.

"There aren't as many refugees as yesterday, but since dawn they have been trickling in. I guess it's still too dangerous to move around at night, but that may change soon."

Caden cocked an eyebrow. "What have you heard?"

"They're working to restore power and the state patrol and local police are back in the area."

Caden recalled a verse he had been taught in Sunday school, "God commanded the light to shine out of darkness." Darkness had spread across the land, but the light was pushing back.

As he leaned against the parapet and watched the people coming, he recalled again the words of the chaplain. "We're like Nehemiah on the wall. Behind us is justice, order and democracy, and in front of you, what we keep out is the enemy—ignorance, tyranny and chaos."

He chuckled. *It's not even Sunday and I'm getting all spiritual and philosophical.* Despite his attempt to dismiss it, the snippets kept coming. *Where there is no vision, the people perish. Who will stand in the gap?* In their own way, both his church pastor and the chaplain had spoken of strengthening what remained of the spirit and ideals that made the country strong.

He shook his head. *Why am I thinking about all of this today?* He felt like a pendulum that had swung from the darkness of last night into the light of the morning sun. Right now his disposition was fine, but he didn't want to swing back.

Then he knew, with a certainty he didn't understand, that he wouldn't swing into darkness. He was where he needed to be, doing what needed to be done. As a younger man he had left home and not looked back, but with the first attack, like a moth to light, he had been drawn toward Hansen. *Perhaps all of us are right where God needs us.* Images of Peter, alive and dead, flashed through his mind. *Was Peter where God needed him? Were the soldiers that died yesterday where they needed to be?*

He didn't know. Perhaps it was unknowable.

A glance at his watch revealed he had been pondering his role in the universe, watching the flow of refugees and the coming and going of soldiers for nearly an hour. *Almost late for the briefing.* He jogged back into the building and to his meeting.

When Caden completed his brief, the general frowned. "Why were you on the recon mission? Why didn't you stay with the main unit and send someone else to command the recon?"

Because I wanted to check my brother's house. Caden tried to think of something witty or inspired, but finally said, "It seemed right at the time."

"General, do you think we got all the terrorists?" Fletcher asked.

"No, but between you and the army Stryker brigade, we believe you got most of them."

Thankful that Fletcher had changed the topic, Caden took a long sip of coffee.

The general studied a paper on his desk. "The army found three wounded jihadists after the battle. The rest were dead. The few that may have escaped are combat ineffective. The State Patrol and other guard units hit the other gangs hard yesterday and will again today.

"South of here, we're restoring power block-by-block and clearing hot spots. Once we've removed the lawless elements from this area, we can begin those tasks here, and move people back. All of Tacoma should have power and water by summer. Who knows, in a few years it may be the state's largest city. Because of the radiation, this base will be the northern limit of habitation, for now."

"What about the Chinese in the port of Tacoma?" Caden took another sip.

The general smiled. "They've been very quiet. We still have army units around them and we've been flying drones over the port. Now that the gangs and terrorists the PLA used are destroyed, we're hoping they decide to leave the northwest. That would free up the army units for the fight against Durant."

"What is next for us?" Caden asked.

"I know you've taken the brunt of this action. I plan to keep you out of the fighting, but I want you available for a couple of days, just in case. I think we can rotate you back to Hansen on Monday."

Caden leaned back in the chair and savored the smell rising from his cup. *We left on Monday and we'll head home on this coming Monday. Eight days.* "Thank you, sir."

Later, when he was alone, Caden was tempted to share the news with Maria, but he knew such information was classified. Still, he could tell her that he was okay and find out how things were in Hansen. Retrieving his phone from the nightstand he pressed the numbers. *No service?* He frowned remembering that the building he was in had power because they hooked up generators. He looked out the window at the dark city. *Cell towers for miles around don't have power.*

He wanted to talk to Maria, to know the news from Hansen. He had been so close to them all, so involved in the struggles of life and his hometown. He sighed and consoled himself with the knowledge that he would be home on Monday. *That will be soon enough.*

*   *   *

"Where is my daughter?"

Zach, in handcuffs, stared across the table at Mr. Hollister. "Like I've been telling everyone, MS-13 has her."

"Because of you!" He spat the word like venom.

Like some soul-killing poison, guilt flowed through Zach. His gaze dropped to the floor. "I…I tried…." His head shot up and he locked eyes with the older man. "No! I avoided Bo and his gangster friends. It was only after the gang shot Bo and took DeLynn that I followed and talked with them. That is what gave me time to do something to save her, but we only have until Sunday—and no will listen to me."

Hollister stood and walked to the door. Then he stopped and looked back at Zach. "I dislike you, but I love my daughter. On the possibility that you might have useful information about DeLynn, I will listen. For once, try to impress me."

CHAPTER TWENTY EIGHT

Maria stacked firewood in the shed while Trevor split the logs just outside. When Nikki barked, she poked her head out to see why. Trevor pointed to a red sedan driving along Hops Road. It was just a curiosity, until it turned up the long driveway.

Trevor jogged toward the front of the house.

Maria went in the backdoor, grabbed a shotgun and stood just inside with it out of view.

A man with silver and black hair stepped from the car. Maria would have said he was in his mid-forties, but his shoulders slumped, his eyes looked tired, and his clothes hung loosely. *Maybe that's the way we all will look soon.*

"Can I help you?" Trevor asked, as the man approached.

Although still a pup, Nikki did her best to growl at the intruder.

"My name is Kent Hollister. Perhaps you know my daughter, DeLynn?"

Trevor shook his head.

Maria thought Caden had mentioned the name.

Well, I represent Zach Brennon. He was arrested yesterday for the murder of Robert Hendricks and…."

"What?" Maria stepped onto the porch.

Trevor invited Kent into the house.

Nikki followed everyone in and lay down next to a jabbering Adam.

Sarah brought their guest a cup of tea and then headed back toward the kitchen door, but stopped as he continued to explain the predicament.

"According to Zach, for my daughter DeLynn to have any

chance of getting out alive, he must meet with MS-13 no later than Sunday morning and deliver a substantial number of weapons.

"The sheriff sent a couple of deputies to check out the ranger station. There were some beer cans and other trash that appeared recent, but little else."

"The sergeant at the armory...." Kent shook his head. "The guy looks young enough to be my kid. Anyway, he said there is nothing he can do."

"The problem is there is no way to verify Zach's story. While the sheriff doesn't have anyone who saw him shoot Mr. Hendricks, the circumstantial case against Zach is strong. I think they could get a conviction."

"You sound like the prosecution, not his lawyer." Maria said.

"I'm just being realistic. When I discussed the facts with him this morning, Zach stated that your family might be of help to him and DeLynn."

Trevor rubbed his chin.

Maria thought, searched for her phone, and then dialed Caden. As it rang, she paced. It went to voice mail. "Caden, Zach has been arrested and DeLynn is missing and in danger. Call me." Then she called Lisa at the hospital. "Is David awake? Can he talk?"

"No. Why?" After Maria explained she said, "I'll ask if he knows how to contact Caden as soon as I can."

After she hung up, Maria continued to pace. "We've got to do something. We can't just let DeLynn be killed."

"What can we do? We don't know where Caden and the soldiers are or when they'll be back," Trevor said.

Sarah sat beside her husband. "The governor knows Caden."

All heads turned to Sarah at once.

"It was just an idea," she said.

Trevor hugged his wife.

*   *   *

Standing on the top of the professional building, Caden saw that the fire in the distant apartment tower was out. Observing the nearby streets he wondered if it had burned out or been put out. Military and police were on patrol. People walked along the roads. Two fire engines were parked in the lot next to the building. South from the base, life was returning to the city.

"You're a hard man to find."

At the sound of the general's voice, Caden turned and saluted. "Just trying to stay out of trouble, sir." He smiled.

"Well, trouble may have found you."

Caden cocked an eyebrow.

"I got a call from the governor this morning…."

"The phones work?"

"Surprised me, too, when I felt something move in my pocket." Harwich pointed to a tower in the distance. "That one came on line this morning. Anyway, the governor ordered your men back to Hansen immediately and says to phone home."

He thanked the General and began a search of his pockets before he remembered leaving the phone by his cot. He ran to his room, turned the device on, but had no service. He ran to the roof. *One bar, two, one.* He noticed a message from Maria and, as he listened, his alarm grew. Zach arrested? DeLynn in danger? He fumbled as he phoned. *It's not ringing.* He dialed again. On the third attempt he heard Maria's voice.

"Caden! We've been trying to get in touch with you since yesterday. I've got so much to tell you. David was shot at the hospital and…."

The call dropped.

Dialing again, he wondered if Brooks was alive. *Did Zach shoot him? Is that why he was arrested? What danger is DeLynn in? Zach wouldn't hurt her.* Caden needed to find Fletcher and get the men ready to leave, but if he left the roof he'd lose the cell signal and he wanted to know more about the situation.

Busy? He sighed in frustration. *She's calling me.* He waited a few seconds, tried again, and she answered.

"If this call fails I'll call you when we get closer to Hansen. We're coming home."

"Great, we really need—"

"Wait. Is David okay?"

"He's out of intensive care. They think he'll be fine."

"Who shot him?"

"One of the MS-13 gang when they moved Cruz."

Caden shook his head recalling the concerns about the girl that visited Cruz and the upcoming move. Now he wished he had acted upon those concerns. "Did Cruz escape?"

"Yes."

He gritted his teeth. "What was Zach arrested for?"

"Murdering Bo. But I don't think he did it."

"I hope not." *But it's certainly within the realm of possibility.*

"There is more we need to talk about. We need to help DeLynn. Zach says…."

Again, the call dropped.

It was frustrating, but except for the DeLynn predicament, Caden felt he had a grasp of the situation and would soon be home and know the full story. He found Fletcher and told him what he knew.

"Sounds like while we've been making Renton and SeaTac safe, home fell apart."

Caden nodded. "Let's head back before things get worse."

As the Hansen convoy pulled away from Camp Victory, Caden stared at his phone screen. *No bars.*

Later as the trucks rumbled south, his phone rang.

"Caden, this is David Weston. Hold for the Governor."

He sat up in the seat.

"Caden?" The governor's voice came through the phone. "Are you on the way to Hansen?"

"Yes, sir." The capitol dome stood in the distance. "We're passing through Olympia right now."

"Great. I wanted to make sure there were no problems detaching your people from the operation and getting you home."

"It went well. We should be there in an hour. Thank you, Governor."

"You should thank Maria. She's a very persistent woman. Yesterday afternoon she pushed through the Byzantine phone tree we have and reached David. After he explained the situation with MS-13 and the young girl…well, I knew you should be home."

"Young girl? DeLynn? What happened? I haven't heard."

"Oh." For several moments there was only silence. "I've been told that a teenage girl was kidnapped and is being held ransom by MS-13. If you need assistance let me know."

When Caden hung up with the governor, he turned to the driver. "Hurry."

*　　　*　　　*

The convoy was just outside of Hansen when Caden ordered it to stop yards from the turn for Hops Road and his family's farm. There was no curb or siding to allow the trucks to pull out of the lane but, since there was no traffic, they just stopped.

Caden walked back to talk with Fletcher. "I've learned more on the way down here." He held up his phone. "Take the men on to the armory and get them ready for…I don't know what, but get them prepared. I'll be there as soon as possible."

"They'll be ready." Fletcher saluted and returned to his vehicle.

While the convoy proceeded toward town, Caden, in his SUV, turned down the side road toward home. His father waited on the front porch as he drove up.

Still in ACUs, and with his helmet on, Caden stepped from the car.

"Hello son. It's good to see you home."

Nikki danced at his feet.

"Hi, Dad." He removed the helmet and tossed it on the passenger seat. His mother burst from the house and embraced him alongside the car.

After hugs and welcomes they moved toward the porch. Caden asked, "Where's Maria?"

"At the hospital," his father said.

"With Brooks? How is he?"

His father's face darkened. "Cruz shot him in the back. Dr. Scott says he'll recover—but it will take time."

Caden took a slow deep breath and resolved to destroy MS-13 and rescue DeLynn.

His mother wrapped her arm around Caden. "But, Maria is probably with Sue."

"Sue? She's in the hospital? What happened to…did she have the baby?"

She smiled. "You have a nephew. She named him Peter. You're Uncle Caden now."

He smiled and then recalled the note in his pocket and the body that would soon be at the armory. "I also have news. I got to Peter and Sue's home and I found Peter." He let that hang in the air for a moment.

His mother's face aged and she clasped her hands as if in prayer.

His father rubbed his chin. "Peter's body?"

"Yes."

His father's face slumped into an older, sadder, version of itself.

Tears rolled down his mother's cheeks.

Caden handed the plastic bag to them.

With his father's arm resting on his mother's shoulder they read the last words of their first born son.

"It's some comfort to know." His father handed the open note back to Caden, but continued to look at the envelope. "I can't imagine what I would say in such a letter."

Several times, before particularly hazardous combat missions, Caden had written a note to his parents. He had seen many soldiers writing similar messages for loved ones. He could imagine what it said, but didn't want to.

He retrieved the bag from his father. "I'll see Sue today. I'm certain she will ask if I got to her house. I'll give her the letter then." He turned to go, but stopped with a sigh. He had just delivered the worst news a parent could receive and now he had to rush off.

"Where is Peter?" his mother asked.

"The convoy took his…he's at the armory." He hugged her. "There is a lot that needs doing and I've got to see a bunch of people."

Near tears once again she held him. "Come back."

"I promise."

Caden drove towards town. The hospital and sheriff's office were about equal distance from where he was. Despite the assurances that he was recovering, he wanted to see Brooks. Also, despite the tears he was certain would follow, he wanted to deliver the letter to Sue and see the new baby. However, the information he needed to destroy MS-13 and save DeLynn was in the other direction.

Next stop, the sheriff's office.

"It's good to see you," the guard said at the entrance to the building. "I suppose you heard about the troubles this week." He buzzed open the door.

"I'm learning," Caden said with a grimace and walked through to the office.

The sheriff looked up from the papers on his desk and blinked. "I really need the deputies to warn me when you come."

"We need to talk and I'd like to see Zach."

"Sure. Good to see you back here in one piece. Have you heard...well, about everything? It's been a busy week."

"Busy for us both." Caden sat down. "Tell me about Bo's murder and why you think Zach is involved."

The sheriff outlined the case against the boy, concluding with, "He marched in here with a stolen rifle."

"Really?"

"The AR-15 he was carrying belonged to a guy who died during the battle outside of town."

Caden rubbed his forehead trying to absorb all the sheriff had told him. "Okay, it doesn't look good, but do you really think Zach killed Bo?"

"I go where the evidence takes me and right now it's taking me to Zach."

"I remember reading once that the first person to speak in court sounds right until they get cross-examined." Caden stood. "I want to clear up a few things—let's go see the boy."

"I need to phone his attorney."

"He has a lawyer?"

"Kent Hollister, DeLynn's father."

Caden tried to get his mind around the idea of the missing girl's father representing the possible kidnapper.

Hoover watched and smiled. "I'll let him explain it to you."

After the call, Hoover led the way. "Normally we would have transferred him to a juvenile facility, but the nearest one isn't taking anyone new, so I did some rearranging and put him in a cell by himself." He shook his head. "The whole juvenile system and Child Protective Services is collapsing. Actually, a lot of things are going to...hey, Douglas, let us in."

The man buzzed them into a part of the building Caden had never seen. He scanned the austere cement and steel room and hoped such visits would remain a rarity.

Hoover seemed not to notice the difference and continued

his rant. "Where was I? Oh, the county told me this morning that we might be late getting paid. That's bad enough, but the money is hardly worth anything. Most of my deputies are having real trouble feeding their families. We'd need a huge pay raise just to keep up with inflation, but do you think we'll get it?" The sheriff looked a Caden.

He shook his head. "I'm in the same boat. The state pays me with the same money you get."

On their left was a line of green steel doors.

Hoover took a deep breath. "I guess I needed to vent. The kid's cell is just up here."

When the sheriff opened the cell door Zach jumped from the bunk. "Major Westmore, I'm innocent, please believe me."

Caden started to ask a question, but Zach continued.

"We've got to act fast if we're going to save DeLynn."

CHAPTER TWENTY NINE

The creak and slam of a steel door announced the arrival of attorney Kent Hollister. The deputy escorted him to where Caden, the sheriff and Zach sat around a simple table in a Spartan visiting room.

"My client has maintained his innocence in the murder of Robert Hendricks and wishes to cooperate in any way possible to prove that and facilitate the safe return of DeLynn Hollister."

Looking at Zach, Caden frowned. "I think your attorney is too personally involved in this case."

Hoover nodded. "I still think he's guilty, but I've said the same thing. He didn't listen to me." He turned to Zach. "Your lawyer wants his daughter back more than your exoneration."

"I told my client I had serious reservations, but—."

"No. Stop." Zach glanced at a clock on the wall. "We have less than twenty hours to find a way to save DeLynn. Hearing what I have to say is the best way to get her back *and* prove I'm innocent. Mr. Hollister has agreed to help me do that. Listen and I'll tell you everything." He took a deep breath. "I was on a rock outcrop across from Bo's house."

"My client was watching an alleged criminal, nothing else." Hollister added.

"One of the MS-13 gang killed Bo's bodyguard." Zach closed his eyes.

"Did you find that body?" Caden asked.

Hoover nodded.

"I heard Bo say to them that he was looking for me. They were going to kill him right there, beside the bodyguard, because he wasn't any use to them. Then Bo told them about my sister, Vicki.

Cruz wanted to find her and they all got in his car and took off for my house. I ran the path over the ridge."

Hoover shook his head. "I said before that it is impossible to run from Hendricks' home to yours and arrive just after they did."

"It was a hard run, but not impossible. I've offered to do it again to show you."

"If you could do it, I certainly couldn't keep up with you," the sheriff said with a smirk.

Zach glanced at the sheriff's paunch and then continued. "I really did arrive just after the gang. I hid in the forest, and saw them drag DeLynn from the house. They think she is my sister. Since they had her, they shot Bo. I tried to aim and—."

"Let's not go into things you didn't do," Hollister said.

"So, DeLynn knows who really killed Bo?" Caden asked.

"Yes! If we rescue her she can tell you. Anyway, the gang drove off with her, that's when I...." Zach looked at his lawyer.

"Zach borrowed my car to pursue the real criminals in this case."

Hoover frowned. "That's not what you said during the 911 call."

"It was all just a misunderstanding."

"Can I go on?" Zach looked around the table and then continued, outlining the conversation he had with Cruz. "I only have until tomorrow at 9:00 in the morning to deliver twenty M4s to Cruz or he kills DeLynn.

"You were caught with a stolen weapon." Hoover said to Zach.

"He was turning himself and the rifle in to you," Hollister countered.

Ignoring the attorney, the sheriff's gaze remained fixed on Zach. "You were seen arguing and threatening Bo Hendricks at Library Park."

"We don't deny it. Mr. Hendricks threatened my client's sister, but Zach did not kill him."

"He was found dead in your driveway."

Hollister again jumped into answer. "According to your own investigation, Mr. Hendricks was on his knees. The assailant stood behind him when he was shot—execution style. How would my client manage that? Also, the bullet was a 9mm. My client doesn't own or possess such a weapon."

Caden held up his hand signaling for everyone to stop. Turning to the sheriff, he said, "We need to talk."

Together they stepped from the room.

"Show me on a map where Zach's and Bo's homes are."

"We'll need to go to the office. There is a big map of the county on the far wall."

Caden had seen the map, but never taken much notice of it. Standing before it he saw all the logging roads, dirt county roads and detailed topography.

Hoover pointed with his index finger. "Bo's house is here." He pressed his thumb to the map. "And Zach's house is here."

Caden looked at the distance between the two points. "Zach said he ran as hard as he could and arrived at his home right after the gang." He rubbed his chin. "I don't see how. He'd either have to run around that ridge or over it."

"He claims he went over it."

"Well then that's it isn't it? If he can do it again, his story is believable, if he can't, it isn't."

Hoover nodded. "What's to keep him from just running off?"

"I think I can find people to keep up with him." He tapped at his phone. "First Sergeant, get the six best runners we have and meet me at the sheriff's office ASAP."

*   *   *

Caden explained to everyone what he wanted and then, drove to Zach's home. When he arrived at the blue single-wide trailer, he realized he didn't know if anyone was there. He climbed the rickety wood porch and knocked on the door. There was no answer. He wondered if the mother was alive or perhaps still in the hospital. He tried the knob, found it locked, and retreated down the stairs.

Pacing the driveway, he decided to text Maria. "Call me when you're alone."

A minute later his phone rang. "Are you in Hansen?" Maria asked. "Why did you want me to be alone when I called?"

"Yes, I'm in Hansen. I'll explain the secrecy in a minute. How's Brooks?"

In a somber tone she said, "He was awake and talking earlier.

184

He should be okay in a few weeks. Did you hear that Sue had her baby? Every day when I visit she asks—."

"Every day? How long has she been in the hospital?"

"Sue had a fever and the baby was jaundiced, but they're both better. I'm supposed to take them home later today. She's been concerned about you, but I think she wants to know if you learned anything about Peter."

"That's why I wanted to make sure you were alone. I did get to their house." He explained that he found Peter's body and a note, but left out most other details.

Maria was silent for a moment. "I wish you hadn't told me. I'm going to be driving her back to the farm in about an hour. How do I sit in the car and talk to her knowing that? What if she asks about you?"

"Sorry. I didn't think of that."

Hoover pulled up and parked behind Caden's car. "I've got to go." he said. "We'll talk later."

Stepping out of the car the sheriff said, "The boy is with your people and is headed over to Bo's house."

*   *   *

The March sun was low on the horizon by the time everyone was in place. Fletcher held the radio to his mouth. "We just arrived at the spot above Bo's house." He looked from the rock outcropping across to home. "Good sniper position."

Zach stood tall and smiled. "I've done a lot of hunting." Then hastily added, "But I didn't shoot Bo."

"I don't think you did." Fletcher turned to face Zach and the six soldiers with them. "Just so everyone is clear, when the deputy waves his arm you guys run. Follow the path over the ridge, but keep going after that. The finish line is Zach's house. Your job is to keep up with Zach. Don't let him out of your sight." He pointed to the deputy below. "He will drive to the house as a kind of pace car. Are you guys ready?"

Zach nodded.

The soldiers shouted, "Hooah" and slapped Zach on the back.

Feeling a gentle hand on his shoulder, Zach turned.

"I'm looking forward to seeing how fast we can do this."

John Tyler said.

"If we're going to find DeLynn, I've got to give it everything I've got."

Tyler grinned. "I'll try to keep up."

Zach focused on the deputy's vehicle, the pace car. He had been asked during his first interrogation if the gang had sped off. Truthfully, he had told them no. The car had driven away at a normal rate of speed. Now he was grateful that fact had come out. The deputy had been told to go the speed limit.

Zach focused on the deputy in front of Bo's house. He was talking on the car radio to someone, probably the people at his trailer. After a moment the deputy stopped and looked in the direction of the rock outcrop.

Zach tensed, ready to run.

The radio crackled. "Go."

The deputy waved his arm.

Zach shot into the forest.

*   *   *

The pace car would be there any second. Caden looked down the driveway with concern. Then from behind came the sound of snapping twigs and limbs.

Zach burst from the forest into the driveway and fell to his knees breathing heavily.

Right behind him was Tyler. "Geez Zach…Olympics…that's what you should do."

Caden showed the sheriff the stopwatch. "It can be done."

As several more soldiers stumbled in, the pace car drove up.

"Okay, the kid's story *could* be true," the sheriff said.

"I think he's telling the truth."

"I am…telling the…truth," a still breathless Zach said as he approached. "Let's find…DeLynn now…okay?"

Caden rested a hand on his shoulder. "Transfer him to military custody while we conduct our operation."

Hoover gave him a confused look. "What kind of operation are you going to do?"

"After we do some planning, Zach is going to call Cruz."

*   *   *

Looking at the notes he had written and considering all the

186

plans they had discussed, Caden was frustrated. For over an hour, with the Sheriff and the First Sergeant, he had been trying to plan an operation to rescue DeLynn and arrest or kill the members of MS-13. They had sent Zach with Hollister to load M4s in the car. The squads were ready, but without knowing the location of the meeting, in-depth planning was impossible.

Dressed in ACUs and with a bow and quiver on his back, Zach walked into the armory office with Kent Hollister. "I've put the rifles in the trunk of the car." He looked at his watch. "We have less than fourteen hours. When do you want me to make the call?"

"We're just about done here, but you can stow the bow. I'm not taking you on a dangerous mission."

Zach took the seat at the table. "MS-13 is expecting me. I have to make the call."

"Call from here. We will handle the rest."

Kent sat beside Zach.

"She's my girlfriend. I thought I was part of the 'we' here at the armory and besides—"

Caden took a slow, deep, breath. "Emotions are a bad thing in this type of operation. Even if you were married to her, I wouldn't want you along. You are part of the armory team, but you are also still a minor."

"MS-13 will probably want to see me."

"Let's hope there is a way we can do this without you standing in the line of fire. Here." Caden handed Zach the phone that Cruz had given him. "Make the call."

Zach frowned, but dialed.

"You got the guns and stuff?" It was Cruz.

"Yes. Put De..." He stopped, remembering that Cruz thought she was his sister. "Put Vicki on the phone."

"Well, the kid is excited to see his sister." Cruz laughed.

Zach heard fumbling and shuffling and then DeLynn's voice as she read, "Zach, go to the ranger station and wait. You'll be told."

The call ended.

"My daughter—she's okay?"

Zach nodded. "I heard her voice." Turning to the others he continued. "They want me to go to the ranger station, but he said earlier that the meeting wouldn't be there. Didn't you guys check it?"

"We did. The place was deserted." Hoover shook his head.

"They're probably sending someone there now." Fletcher added. "They might even want him to show the rifles so whoever is watching can see, and then they'll say where the meeting will be."

Caden gave a reluctant nod.

"Zach needs to go there and find out where the meeting is," Hollister said.

Zach is seventeen. Private Conner was eighteen. Conner was my responsibility, but now he's dead. He stared at Zach. *I won't have two kids die in this craziness in a single week.*

"What?" Zach asked with eyes fixed on Caden. "Why are you staring at me?"

Caden rubbed his forehead. "There is no way you're going on this operation."

"Can we talk about this?"

"We just did."

"In normal times using a minor just wouldn't happen, but these are not normal times." Hoover leaned back in the chair. "If Zach does not show up at the ranger station with the guns, we may never find out where the meeting is supposed to take place."

Caden looked at Hoover with surprise. "You've been saying he's guilty, now you want to give Zach guns and send him on his way to a criminal gang. How you changed your mind about him?"

Hoover sighed and stared at Zach. "Yeah, I guess I have."

"I've always thought Zach was innocent," Fletcher said, "but are we really discussing sending one kid on a very dangerous mission to try and save another kid?"

"That other kid is my daughter," Hollister said.

Hoover threw up his hands in frustration. "If we stand any chance of getting these guys…"

"Or rescuing DeLynn," Zach added emphatically.

"…we probably need Zach along at least."

"No," Caden said.

"What else can we do?" Hollister asked.

"While you guys argue I need to use the latrine." Zach walked from the room.

Fletcher rubbed his chin. "What if there was a way to bring

him along, but keep him out of the line of fire?"

"How?" Caden asked.

"Keep him in the shadows," Fletcher said.

"Yeah, we only need his voice," Hoover added.

Five minutes later Caden nodded reluctantly. "This might work, but Zach stays with me until Cruz and the others are dead."

"Okay," Hoover said.

"Where is Zach?" Fletcher asked.

After they checked the nearby latrine, Fletcher phoned the gate guard.

"Yeah he left the base about ten minutes ago in that car he's been driving lately."

Fletcher turned to Hollister. "You gave Zach the keys to your car?"

"He asked for them to load the rifles."

Caden gritted his teeth. "Phone Zach. Let's see if we can get him to come back."

As Fletcher did, Caden said, "Put him on speaker."

"Zach what are you doing?" Fletcher slid the phone to the center of the table.

"I'm going to find out where the meeting is, and then I'll phone you and tell you the location."

"Zach, turn around and come back." Caden ordered with an angry voice. "What's to keep MS-13 from killing you, and taking the weapons when you arrive at the ranger station?"

"Well, besides my bow, I've got one of the rifles beside me, but I'm hoping they play this deal straight."

"You're hoping MS-13 will be honest?" Hoover asked.

"Yeah, I guess I am, but unless you have a better plan, this is the one I'm going with."

No one spoke for a moment. Zach had forced their hand and Caden now considered options that he had been unwilling to explore moments before. "Zach, maybe there is better plan."

*   *   *

Zach parked in front of a dark ranger station. The moon was nearly full, but clouds obscured its light. He looked to either side. *I could be surrounded by MS-13 and not know it.* He tried to breathe normal and remain calm. *What have I gotten myself into?*

From out of the darkness came a female voice. "Get out of the car."

CHAPTER THIRTY

"Did you hear me?"

Despite the youthfulness of her voice, it carried authority and a Hispanic accent that caused Zach's stomach to knot. *Does MS-13 have female members?* Looking to his left, he squinted, but saw nothing in the darkness.

"Are you deaf? Open the door and get out!" She cursed.

He glanced at the rifle leaning against the passenger seat and realized it was useless. He couldn't hide it. Unarmed, he opened the car door and stepped out.

"Keep your hands where I can see them. You got the stuff?"

Unable to speak, he nodded.

"Show me."

He swallowed. "There's one against the passenger seat." He leaned toward the door to retrieve the weapon.

"Leave it there. Where are the others?"

"The rest are in the trunk." He stepped to the back.

The female inched from the darkness into the pale moonlight. It was difficult to see detail, but her hair was long, straight and dark. She appeared to be no more than a few years older than him. Zach's gaze snapped from her face to the pistol she waved at him.

"Open the trunk." She gestured with the gun.

Zach complied.

"Move away."

As he retreated she approached the car and used a flashlight to look over the weapons.

"It's all there, just like Cruz wanted. Where's De…my sister?"

Zach needed to be careful. He still wasn't sure it would help, but since they thought they had Vicki, he might as well let them continue to believe it.

"Give me the phone they gave you."

He pulled it from his pocket and stepped toward her.

"Put it on the car!" She stepped back.

He did as told.

She picked up the phone, taped on the screen and spoke Spanish.

Zach wished he had paid more attention in school, he barely understood three words.

When done, she looked at Zach. "Up this road is a cabin—."

"The ranger cabin. I know it."

"Good, go there now," she said backing into the darkness.

Zach returned to the Hollister car and drove up the gravel logging road about a half-mile. Then he stopped, pulled a phone from under the car seat, and called Caden. "I'm clear. Did you get that girl I talked to?"

"Yes, we have her in custody. Where are you? The squad said you drove up the logging road."

Zach told him the meeting would be at an old ranger log cabin several miles up the forest service road. "But there's something important you need to know. This road connects with two others that go to the next county, but they cross over high ridgelines."

He heard the rustle of paper over the phone. "If Cruz just looked at a map he probably thinks he has three ways out, but he doesn't. Those other roads are snowbound this time of year."

"Got it," Caden said. "Someone will join you in a minute. Wait where you are."

Nothing moved in the headlights. Within seconds Zach mumbled, "Come on. Where are you?"

A knock sounded on the passenger side window.

Zach stifled a scream, and then unlocked the door.

"Hi." John Tyler reached in and unlocked the back door of the sedan. "Let the Major know I'm with you." In full combat gear and with an M4, his friend climbed into the back seat. "I'll stay back here till you get close to the cabin."

"Corporal Tyler is with me," Zach said into the phone.

"Good. Take it slow so our men can deploy, but don't go too

slow."

Zach wondered what speed that would be.

Tyler handed him a pistol. "I thought you might need this. When you meet I suggest you make sure they see the M4, but keep the pistol hidden. Shove it down your pants."

The pistol was the smallest Zach had ever seen. "Down my pants? I don't want a gun pointed there."

Tyler laughed. "Just don't pull the trigger."

"What kind of gun is this?"

"A Ruger LCP. It's my sister's. She keeps it in her purse."

"So the Major doesn't know you're giving this to me?"

Tyler shook his head.

Very gently Zach slid the gun into his pants and then shifted the vehicle into drive.

The car rolled forward with a thud as it went over a rock.

Zach stopped the vehicle. Eased the gun from his pants and set it on the passenger seat.

"What am I sitting on?" Tyler said from the back seat. "Oh. Why did you bring the bow and quiver?"

He shrugged. "It's what I usually hunt with."

Tyler squeezed Zach's shoulder. "Good hunting tonight."

Several bumps farther along, Tyler asked, "Are you sure you're on the road? It doesn't feel like it."

"On the road," Zach muttered only vaguely aware of what was said. Though he knew it was several miles away, on every sharp turn he arched his neck hoping for a glimpse of the cabin and DeLynn. His heart pounded in his chest as he fought the fear induced urge to go slower than Caden had advised.

However, he wanted to find and rescue DeLynn. Gradually his speed increased until he hit a rough spot and the car bottomed out on a rock.

Remembering what Caden had told him, he slowed his upward climb.

Please God, keep her safe.

Now, high on the ridge, the air was cold. Snow clung to the ground and stood in drifts in shady spots under trees and in gullies along the road.

The phone buzzed.

Zach jerked.

"Calm down," Tyler said. "No reason to be nervous—yet. Answer the phone."

Zach stopped the car. "Hello?"

"The squads will be in place in a couple of minutes." Caden said. "Go on to the cabin, but don't hang up the phone. Stay outside and stick to the plan."

A few hundred yards from the cabin he stopped, and Tyler darted into the woods.

Zach's stomach flipped and flopped. *God help me help her.* He eased the car forward.

Seconds later he stopped, stepped from the car, and while casually putting on a jacket, slid the cold Ruger deep into the front of his pants. He pushed from his mind the direction of the barrel and zipped up his coat to further conceal it. Then he reached back into the car, grabbed the rifle and stood on the far side of the vehicle with the engine block between him and the ranger cabin.

In the darkness the tiny structure appeared to be sitting alone in a small clearing, but Zach knew that along the east side was a steep drop off. In the daylight, a huge expanse of forest was visible that only stopped at the mountains on the horizon. Where he was on the west side, and on the north, there was a small meadow. On the south side, the forest came up close to the building.

Through a single front window a dim light shone from the cabin. Zach looked, but detected no movement.

His mouth was dry and his stomach ached. He felt like an animal in a snare. He wished he was there for any other reason.

A thought burst to life in his mind. No longer was he a boy just making it from day to day. He was a man on a mission. If tonight was his time to die, then so be it. He would do so as a man, doing what needed to be done to save someone he loved. "Cruz, this is Zach. I'm here with the guns."

Behind him he heard the cock of a pistol.

"Cruz would like you to join him—inside. Leave the gun here."

He leaned it against the car. "Where's my sister?"

"Take off the coat."

The voice was right behind him. Two burly guys approached

from each side.

Zach removed the jacket slowly, hoping the soldiers were in position.

One gang member examined his coat while the other frisked him, but not well. He found Zach's phone and passed it to another. The loss of the phone meant plan 'B' was no longer an option.

Zach hadn't held out much hope that the phone would remain on him, but was pleased when the man didn't go near his groin.

Plan 'A' had been to stay outside where the soldiers could see him and hopefully get DeLynn with him. They had discussed several scenarios in which the soldiers would open fire on the gang, but events seemed to be diverging from the plan.

Zach tried again to find where DeLynn was and was again ignored. "There's one rifle by the passenger seat. The rest are in the trunk." He stepped toward the back. "Let me show you."

A firm hand grasped his arm. "We'll check them out. You've got a meeting with Cruz," the voice from behind said.

One of the men tossed Zach's coat back to him.

"Let's go."

Shoved from behind, Zach stumbled. Regaining his balance, he noticed two others near the trunk of the car and several more at the edge of the forest. *How many people are here?* Since he had been told to get twenty M4s he thought that might be the number. *Is this the whole gang?* Doubt crept in him. *Can I save DeLynn or is this the night we both die?*

Was she inside? If so the soldiers needed to know her location and his, but how would he signal them?

As he climbed the creaking steps, his escort pushed Zach again. "Open the door. Go inside."

The cabin was an old log structure with a main area and one bunkroom. There was no bathroom, just a fairly new outhouse nearby. Cruz sat alone on the far side of the first room. A kerosene lamp cast the gangster in sinister shadows. A woodstove burned in the corner.

The cabin was furnished with four plain wooden chairs, two end tables, and a homemade coffee table. In the corner was a small dining table. The back door was nearby and beside it the door to the bunkroom. All the walls were made of logs, even the interior one that separated the two rooms.

Food containers and beer bottles littered the place, and it smelled of cigarettes and booze.

Before leaving, the escort passed Zach's phone to Cruz.

The gang leader dropped it on the end table next to him, beside another phone.

Zach tried not to look at it, but was glad to know that plan 'B' might still be available and Caden might still hear what was going on. *If it is still on.*

Tyler would use his radio to report the positions of everyone outside, but Zach wasn't outside. If the phone was still on, Caden should know where he was, but what if it wasn't? Did Tyler see him go in? Where was DeLynn? There was no plan 'C,' so it was time to improvise. "Do I get to see my sister now?"

"Why you all dressed in camouflage, boy?"

"The unit just came back from some major operation. I was on duty helping put away the weapons. I'm sure they already know they're missing so let's hurry. Okay?"

"Sure."

"Where is she?"

Cruz shook his head. "In a minute. When I know you got what I asked for." He pointed to a seat.

Zach sat on the far side of the small room with the coat on his lap. He felt the gun through it. "This private pow-wow is so your guys can count guns?" He hoped Caden heard his words through the phone and noticed the word "private."

"Yes," Cruz said.

Seconds ticked slowly by as they sat in silence.

"How long does it take them to count to twenty?" Zach asked.

Cruz smiled, but didn't respond.

A short scraping sound came from the next room. It could have been a rat scratching at something or a chair moving. He strained to hear more.

A phone rang.

Afraid that it was his, Zach felt sick.

From the table beside him, Cruz picked up the other phone

and spoke Spanish. Setting it back down back he said, "My guys tell me there are twenty rifles and magazines, but no bullets."

"The ammo is my insurance."

Cruz smiled. "I like you, kid. I may have to kill you, but I like you. Now where's the bullets?"

Zach's heart pounded. "Where is my sister?"

Cruz's face grew dark.

Zach's heart pounded in his chest. He struggled to keep his voice even. "I have the ammo, but if you kill me you'll never find it."

"There are worse things than death, amigo."

He struggled to sound calm. "Tell me where she is and I'll tell you where the ammo is."

Cruz stared at him with cold eyes. Then he made a slight movement of the head in the direction Zach had heard the noise.

He hurried to the bunk room with Cruz right behind.

For a moment he didn't notice her. Lit by a single candle on an ancient dresser by the door, half the tiny room was cast in dark shadows. A bunk bed stood against the outer wall with blankets hanging down. Beyond that, in the corner was DeLynn, bound tight to a chair with a cloth sack over her head.

Zach ran to her side, removed the sack and the gag that was under. "Did they hurt you?"

She shook her head.

"I did my part," Cruz said. "No one touched her, but now it's time to do your part and tell me where the rest of the stuff is or…things change—for both of you."

Zach kissed her on the forehead and then on the lips.

Cruz made a disgusted noise. "I've heard about you country people marrying your cousins, but…."

Remembering that MS-13 believed that she was his sister, he laughed. "We're very close."

Cruz spat on the floor. Then cast Zach a doubtful look. "Whatever. Where's the bullets?"

The phone in the next room rang.

The thug cursed, turned and left.

Zach untied DeLynn's hands.

She worked to free her legs.

From the next room Cruz called out. "My friends say there's

a bow in the back seat."

Zach reached down the front of his pants.

DeLynn's face was a mixture of surprise and confusion.

He retrieved the gun and raced to the edge of the door.

"You live close to the spot where someone shot me with an arrow."

Zach heard the floorboards creak as Cruz marched toward the bunkroom.

"Are you a good shot with the thing?"

"Yes, I'm very good with a bow."

Seeing a shadow in the doorway, he threw his jacket as a decoy.

Shots rang out.

Zach stepped into the doorway and fired a single shot at Cruz. "Bunkroom," he shouted and flung himself against the log wall. When he didn't hear a scream or a thud he knew he didn't hit Cruz, but hoped the phone was still on and that Caden heard him.

Cruz fired wildly splintering the doorframe inches from Zach.

DeLynn screamed, fell on her side, screamed again and continued to untie herself.

Zach was only six feet from her. He wanted to help, but needed to stay by the door.

Three shots, from different sides of the cabin, rang out.

Sniper fire.

A gun battle erupted outside.

Zach needed to be sure the soldiers knew their location.

Cruz cursed. "I'm going to skin you alive, boy." The yellow light of the kerosene lamp vanished, leaving the main room in darkness.

Zach blew out the candle on the dresser. Only moonlight illuminated the struggle.

A bullet ripped through the doorframe mere inches from his hand. From one dark room Zach peeked into another.

Yelling in Spanish, a man burst in through the front door.

Right behind another screamed, fell through the door and then regained his footing. Blood stained his side.

They both knelt and fired into the night.

Zach fired at each.

The second man slumped to the floor.

The other gang member dashed for cover.

As he did Zach fired again and wondered how many rounds were left in the pistol.

CHAPTER THIRTY ONE

Zach struggled to remember each shot, but he didn't know if the clip had been full when Tyler gave it to him. He wasn't sure how many rounds it held. *Six, maybe seven.* To be sure he'd have to remove the clip and count, but he didn't want to disarm himself with a crazy killer in the next room.

Pale moonlight flowed through a small window at the end of the bunkroom and brought Zach a ray of hope. When DeLynn freed herself from the ropes, Zach pointed to the window and whispered, "Open it." Then he gestured she should jump out.

She nodded and pushed to open it.

Seeing that she couldn't budge it, Zach kept an eye on the door as he stepped back toward her. Together they pushed and it moved.

"You can get it now. I need to stay by the door. Oh, there's a cliff just a few feet beyond the window so jump straight down and run south—"

"A cliff? South? Which way is that?"

"With your back to the building it would be on your right."

She nodded. "You're coming too?" It was a question and a plea.

"I will, but first I'll cover you and then follow. Don't wait for me; go as soon as you can."

Zach hurried back to the door as the gunfire continued. He dropped to the floor and crept past the edge of the dresser trying to see what had happened. The front door stood half open. The man Zach had shot lay crumpled near the window. A trail of blood marked his crawl to where he died. He wondered why the other gang members hadn't helped him.

In the midst of danger Zach allowed himself only a moment to feel the gravity of taking a life. Then he shoved it to the back of his mind to be dealt with later.

"The window is still stuck." DeLynn said in a loud whisper.

"Push. You can do it." Then he looked for Cruz and the other thug, but didn't see them. He had one, maybe two bullets left, so he either wanted a way out or a definite target. He inched farther into the doorway.

The steps outside creaked.

Red dots danced along the wall looking for targets.

The front door burst open.

A soldier fired multiple bursts.

Others fired in the windows spraying shards of glass.

Shots boomed from the other side of the wall.

The soldier stumbled toward the bunkroom and fell next to him.

Even in the dim light, Zach recognized John Tyler.

Grabbing his friend's uniform he pulled him into the bunkroom as the gunfight continued. Struggling to contain his growing panic, he felt for a pulse. There was none. Zach stared into Tyler's lifeless eyes as tears welled in his own.

Turning his pistol toward the main room he wiped his eyes. There would be a time for sorrow, but this was not it.

Zach pressed his hand on one of old timbers. *Where is Cruz?* Probably on the *other side of this wall, but I can't shoot him and he can't shoot me through these logs.*

If the gunfire stopped he would dart to the front door and announce who he was, but the pace increased after Tyler was hit. He couldn't see anyone shooting from the cabin. *Did Cruz and the other guy run into the woods?* He wasn't sure.

He had an idea. "DeLynn wait." Grabbing the sling, he pulled the M4 from Tyler. Now that he was better armed, perhaps it was best to remain in the bunkroom. He turned to the window.

It was open and DeLynn was gone.

He leaned out the window. The moonlight was ample to see the narrow path ten feet below. He hadn't remembered it being such a distance down. He squinted to see as much as he could of the gray and black world outside. *Did she jump? Did she fall down the slope?*

"Come on!"

Startled he nearly fell. It was DeLynn near the corner of the building.

He was trying to decide if he should somehow get her back in or join her outside when gunfire near the front of the cabin convinced him to jump.

He tossed the Ruger to her and then the M4. He tried to jump from the window, but it was more of a fall. Hitting the ground with a thud, he moaned, rolled to his feet and ran to DeLynn.

Her lips quivered as if to say something, her eyes pleaded, but no words came forth.

He held her tight. "We're almost safe." He took the M4 from her. "Keep the pistol."

She shook her head. "How does it work?"

"Point and pull the trigger. That'll do for now, but it only has one or two bullets left. He gestured toward the forest that nearly touched the south wall of the cabin. "Go that way. Stay low. I'm right behind you."

Together they ran into the woods.

It was darker in the forest, but Zach was only inches from her. He was about to say that he should lead when, with a thud, he bumped into her. "Why did you stop?" he whispered.

Then he saw Cruz with a pistol an inch from her head.

Zach snapped the M4 to his shoulder and aimed at Cruz.

They were so close their gun barrels nearly touched.

Clouds parted and moonlight flowed through the canopy of trees. Zach recognized the small clearing. The outhouse stood a few yards to the right, the cliff loomed just beyond the trees and brush to his left. If help were to come, they would come from the direction of the outhouse. Zach stepped left, putting the cliff behind him.

Cruz countered by stepping right. The outhouse was now behind him. "Don't do nothing stupid boy. I will kill her. I only need one of you to get me out of here."

Just a few yards away Zach heard the soldiers burst into the cabin and call out his name and DeLynn's. If they had stayed the ordeal would be over. Inwardly he sighed.

"How are you going to get out of here?" Zach asked.

"Walk?"

"I'll do the thinking. There's more than one way out of here."
He stepped closer and pressed the gun to DeLynn's head.

God give me wisdom enough to save her.

"Put down the rifle, boy."

"No."

DeLynn moaned.

Cruz scowled. "All of my brothers are dead because of you.
Do you think I won't kill you?"

"I think you'll kill both of us. That's why I'm not going to
give up the rifle."

"Before I kill you, tell me, is my sister Carina alive?"

"The girl at the ranger station? Yeah, I'm...we're not like you.
We didn't kill her."

The slightest hint of relief crossed the thug's face.

"But you've killed at least one friend of mine tonight."

Coldness filled Cruz's eyes. "Good."

Tree branches snapped.

Zach glanced toward the outhouse.

Cruz grabbed the barrel of Zach's rifle and yanked it up and
to the side.

Trying to keep hold, Zach fired a long burst into the treetops.
Then it stopped and he knew he was out of ammo.

A smile grew across Cruz's face. "I may not get to skin you
alive, but I will kill you."

The crunch of feet in frozen snow told Zach soldiers were
near. He was tempted to shout their location. He knew if he did,
Cruz would make it his last act.

Near the outhouse a soldier stepped into the clearing.

It was Caden.

The gang leader's arms and eyes darted wildly. He fired.

Caden stumbled backward.

Cruz jerked the gun back to Zach and smiled.

Zach stepped back.

A shot thundered in his ears.

He clutched his chest. *Where am I hit?*

Then he saw the growing dark stain on Cruz's shirt.

He snatched the gun from the thug's hand as he collapsed.

"Are you okay?" Zach shouted to Caden. "Medic!"

"I'm okay," Caden said, "he missed."

Fletcher and others came into the clearing from all sides.

The medic checked Cruz and then shook his head.

Zach smiled as Caden approached. "Thanks. You saved my life."

"I didn't get off a shot," Caden said.

Zach looked at the other soldiers.

They shook their heads.

"Then who shot him?" Zach asked.

"I...I did." DeLynn whispered.

CHAPTER THIRTY TWO

DeLynn stared at the lifeless eyes of Cruz. Conversations buzzed around her, but they seemed distant and irrelevant. The Ruger Zach gave her now hung loosely by her side.

Someone stepped close. "I'll take the pistol back."

Zach's voice cracked her isolation. "Is it over?" she asked.

Zach glanced at Caden.

He nodded.

"Yeah we're fine now. Come on let's get out of here." He unwrapped her fingers from the weapon and, gently taking her hand, led her to the clearing.

*   *   *

Still in uniform, Caden stepped from the sheriff's office into the light of morning. It was Sunday and the clear blue sky promised that this day would live up to its name. He tried to figure out how many hours he had been awake, but such effort required more mental focus than he currently possessed. He gave up.

Despite his fatigue, he smiled as he walked across the parking lot toward his car. Cruz was dead. Most of his gang had preceded him or were in jail. DeLynn was home. Zach was free.

There would be a time to honor those who died last night, and earlier this week, but right now he needed to get home before he fell asleep. This morning he was grateful for the lack of traffic the monetary collapse had brought.

He glanced at his watch. *The family will be at the church by now. Probably praying for everyone's safety.*

Even though he wanted nothing more than sleep, he headed toward the church, and his family. He wanted to let them know he was safe and the mission was successful. He also had a duty to let Sue

205

know about Peter and the letter.

With the window down and the radio loud, he stayed awake for the short drive. As he walked into the church, he wondered if Sue had come. *Since she has a baby, and someone will need to keep watch over the farm, she might have chosen to stay home.* He sighed. *And this probably isn't the best place to tell her she's a widow and then hand her a letter with the last words of her husband.* I should have gone home.

Standing in the lobby he heard the pastor.

"The Bible tells us that God blesses those who persevere under trial. To them He has promised the crown of life."

Not wanting to interrupt the sermon and wondering what he would do if Sue were inside, he sat on a nearby bench.

From the sanctuary came the pastor's voice. "God did not bring us these trying times. Wicked men, listening to the author of evil, brought this upon us."

Caden's head slumped forward. *I'll rest my eyes for a moment.*

Soft fingers entwined with Caden's. His eyes blinked open and gazed upon Maria's smile. "Let's go home."

"Is Sue here?"

"No, she's at home with little Peter."

As Maria and Caden crossed the lobby, they were joined by his father and mother. "Where's Lisa?"

"David is out of danger, so she came home last night to get some proper rest. She's looking after the farm and Adam."

As they stepped in the cool air outside, Caden said, "Zach and DeLynn are safe."

Maria squeezed his hand. "Good. Give me the keys."

He awoke when Maria came to a stop in the driveway. His father and mother pulled alongside in the family pickup.

The front door opened and Sue walked onto the porch holding her son. When she saw Caden a hint of expectant hope crossed her face.

Maria moved between Caden and Sue. "He's really tired. Perhaps he can talk when he wakes."

Caden continued toward the house, climbed the four steps to the front porch, and embraced Sue. He wanted nothing more than a few hours of sleep, but he knew he couldn't until he spoke to her. "Come on inside. We need to talk."

She sat on the living room couch and cradled her child close. Caden sat across from her. "I found Peter."

Worry faded from her eyes, replaced by sadness. "Where?"

"He died from radiation sickness in the bedroom of your home."

She shuddered. "I should have stayed…should have been there…I could have helped him."

"No. I don't think that is what he wanted. He knew he was dying when he got there—"

Her eyes widened. "How could you know that?"

Caden pulled the bag with the notes from his pocket.

Sue passed her baby to Maria and began to read.

Tears welled in Sue's eyes, and then ran down her cheeks. Sobs followed. She ran from the room clutching the notes.

Despite what it looked like, Caden hoped that the notes would someday give comfort. He thought of all the bodies they had brought back from Operation Lexington. There were letters he needed to write and wives, mothers, sons and daughters, who would need comfort. However, for now, all necessary duties were completed. He went upstairs to his room for much needed rest.

*   *   *

Monday was a day to honor those who had fallen.

Near an ancient Douglas fir tree on the far side of the Westmore farm, Caden and his father dug a grave. Nearby were the stone markers for his grandparents, an uncle and two aunts.

The morning sun was still below the trees, the air cool, but sweat dripped from the bow of both men.

Caden paused from shoveling and took a pocket knife. With it he punctured each of three blisters that had formed on his hands. As he put away the knife, he heard footsteps. Turning he saw Hoover approach with a shovel.

"Do you need help?" the sheriff asked.

"Your presence is welcome," Caden's dad said, "but you don't have to dig."

Hoover looked into the shallow hole. "Peter was an officer of the law and a friend. I want to help."

Minutes later Fletcher and four others from the armory arrived with Peter's body.

"Friends and neighbors are gathering at your house," Fletcher said. "We thought it best to come directly here."

"I didn't know others would come," Caden said.

Hoover threw a shovel full of dirt from the hole. "This is a small town. Word gets around."

Taking turns, the eight men soon completed the digging.

Trevor went to the house for family and friends as the men lowered the body into the grave.

Caden looked into the earth where his brother lay. He wanted to shout and shake his fist at God. Why did so many good people, like his brother, have to die in the fight against evil? Why couldn't criminals and thugs be the only ones doing the fighting and dying? But he knew the answer. If evil men were fought by those who were equally wicked the only result would be more evil. For good to prevail the good must fight and some would die. The fault didn't lie with God, but with the author of evil.

As dozens of solemn figures walked across the field, Caden looked up from the cold earth into the sunny sky. *Did you choose me to lead the fight here?* He knew the answer.

*   *   *

Zach looked down a long line of battlefield crosses. *So many.* Several others had arranged those crosses, but he had requested to prepare this one.

Civilians gathered along the edge of the parade ground. He saw Vicki, DeLynn, Mr. Hollister, and Maria, but he acknowledged none of them as he moved to the far end of the field.

He retrieved an M-4 and bayonet from the bag. Locking the blade in place he carefully pressed the weapon into the soft earth so that it stood perfectly vertical. He placed the helmet on the stock and the boots to either side.

It seemed proper that he prepare the cross for John Tyler, but despite feeling it was right, tears welled in his eyes.

Fletcher stood at attention not far from him as soldiers marched onto the field. Guests were sitting. The service would begin soon, but he had one final duty to perform before then. Stepping back three paces he snapped to attention. "Thank you for being there. Your courage saved DeLynn and me. Goodbye friend."

Slowly he saluted his fallen comrade.

GLOSSARY

ACU   Army Combat Uniform

AK-47   The AK-47 is a selective-fire military rifle, developed in the USSR, but also used by the People's Republic of China.

Fueler   An army or National Guard fuel truck

Humvee   High Mobility Multipurpose Wheeled Vehicle (HMMWV), commonly known as the Humvee, is a four-wheel drive military vehicle.

JBLM   Joint Base Lewis-McChord (JBLM) is a large military installation located nine miles south-southwest of Tacoma in Washington state.

M11   United States military designation for the SIG P228 pistol. See SIG P228.

M2   The M2 is a Browning .50 caliber machine gun.

M4   The M4 is a common U.S. military magazine-fed, selective fire, rifle with a telescoping stock.

M9   The M9 is a semiautomatic, 9mm, pistol in common use by the United States military.

M35   A military truck in the 2½ ton weight class, often referred to as a "deuce and a half."

MOPP Level   MOPP is an acronym for "Mission Oriented Protective Posture" and as used in the book it refers to the level of protective gear used by military personnel in a chemical, biological, radiological, or nuclear combat situation. MOPP Level zero means gear will be carried, but not worn.

MRE   Meals, Ready-to-Eat (MRE) are self-contained, individual military field rations.

OPLAN Operation Plan

Op Order   Operations Order often abbreviated as OPORD

PLA   The People's Liberation Army of the People's Republic of China

Recon   Military slang for reconnaissance.

RPG   Rocket-propelled grenade

SIG P228   A compact pistol in use with many law enforcement agencies and the military where it is designated as the M11. Caden is given a M11, 9mm .40 S&W, in Chapter 13 along with two 15 round magazines. Caden refers to the M11 by the SIG name.

ALSO BY THE AUTHOR

Through Many Fires
(Strengthen What Remains book 1)
Terrorists smuggle a nuclear bomb into Washington D.C. and detonate it during the State of the Union Address. Army veteran and congressional staffer Caden Westmore is in nearby Bethesda and watches as a mushroom cloud grows over the capital. The next day, as he drives away from the still burning city, he learns that another city has been destroyed and then another. America is under siege. Panic ensues and society starts to unravel.

*   *   *

Titan Encounter   Justin Garrett starts one morning as a respected businessman and ends the day a fugitive wanted by every power in the known universe. Fleeing with his 'sister' Mara and Naomi, a mysterious woman from Earth Empire, their only hope of refuge is with the Titans, genetically enhanced soldiers who rebelled, and murdered millions in the Titanomachy War. Hunted, even as they hunt for the Titans, the three companions slowly uncover the truth that will change the future and rewrite history.

*   *   *

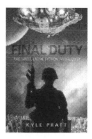

Final Duty – The Speculative Fiction Anthology
Twenty years after the death of her father during the Battle of Altair, Lieutenant Amy Palmer returns to the system as an officer aboard the reconnaissance ship Mirage. Almost immediately disaster strikes and Amy, along with the crew of the Mirage, must face the possibility of performing their final duties. Final Duty is a military science fiction anthology that includes a novella and two short stories set in the same genre and universe.

ABOUT THE AUTHOR

Kyle Pratt is the bestselling author of speculative and science-fiction books. He grew up in the mountains of Colorado. When money for college ran low he enlisted in the United States Navy. While serving on various ships he wrote military science fiction and short stories. After retiring, Kyle taught Yupik Eskimo students in the Alaskan village of Eek for seven years. During the cold nights, he wrote his first full-length novel, *Titan Encounter* and then *Through Many Fires*.

Today, he lives with his wife, Lorraine, of over thirty-six years on a small farm in western Washington state where he writes full-time.

You can learn more about Kyle Pratt at http://www.kylepratt.me

Made in the USA
Lexington, KY
21 February 2015